In the Name of Sin

BOOK ONE, PART ONE OF THE LOVE & SIN SAGA

A novel by
B.R. GREENLEY

Copyright © 2023 B.R. Greenley
All rights reserved
First Edition

NEWMAN SPRINGS PUBLISHING
320 Broad Street
Red Bank, NJ 07701

First originally published by Newman Springs Publishing 2023

ISBN 979-8-88763-753-2 (Paperback)
ISBN 979-8-88763-754-9 (Digital)

Printed in the United States of America

FOREWORD

The dark world of the Immortals is not only fraught with dangers for mortals but for Immortals alike, the demonic deal in half-truths and bold lies. Trust is something that is rarely given and usually exploited, thus leading one to the grave. Respect is taken and never given, and only power itself is wholly respected. In order to truly understand this world, one must look beyond the lies and see the truth that is buried within them, as if hidden in plain sight. The only way to survive the darkness this world is governed by is to embrace it utterly and become part of it.

Seth Maspeth
Great Patron of House Maspeth, Third House of Lust

PROLOGUE

September 3, 1962, Manhattan, New York

Through the gloom of a rapidly dimming candlelight of an old small Victorian bedroom came the subtle sounds of short breaths and labored moans. There on a diminutive but ornately carved bed of brass and wood, perched above her lover, was a nude but beautiful raven-haired woman. Her lustrous rose tattoo upon her back glistened with sweat and stood out among the low light of many candles. She lowered her head toward the man below her, and her lips, still showing signs of makeup, spread into a wide smile.

One of the candles sputtered out, further darkening the room; and her deep blue eyes for a moment gazed toward where the light once was, and it now only showed a wisp of smoke. Her gleaming eyes then looked down again, and her grin widened once more.

"Now's the time, my friend, we have come so far, but we must risk more. If you want me in your life, we cannot fail now," she said softly into his ear, and her grin faded slowly as she spoke.

As her head arched slightly back, and her lower jaw twitched roughly, a loud cracking noise filled the room as it dislocated. Her tongue slowly extended past her lips and lengthened slowly, only to split and give her a great viperlike appearance.

From between the fork of her long tongue, slowly an ivory-colored sharp fang emerged from her flesh; and from the tips of her twin tongues, two smaller fangs extended with a light snap of an unholy pincer. She then lowered her head toward the man still beneath her, enjoying what he thought was a tender moment. The large sharp fang brushed against the soft flesh of his throat, and he twitched in ecstasy at that moment. Slowly the large fang of her tongue slid into the soft flesh of his chest, and he moaned in delight as it dug in deeper. The two smaller fangs latched on to his skin, grasping tightly as the larger one bored farther into his flesh, then it stopped as if it had found its mark, his heart!

She lowered her head and closed her eyes, slowly feeding upon his very life force, and began to drain him steadily but with purpose, but she was fighting hard to keep control. The tissue around the wound pulsated and discolored slightly as the very life energy was siphoned away. It was in that moment her body spasmed once again as her heart shifted from pumping her blood to extracting his life energy. The man gripped the sheets tightly as she continued to drink deeply, and her skin began to pulsate slightly as well now. It was merely moments before she began to slow once again, but with deft speed, she sliced her own wrist with long black talonlike claws that had extended from her fingernails. All the while, she was gripping his wound tightly with her tongues' fangs to stem the flow of his life energy temporarily.

Quickly she thrust her slowly bleeding wrist of thick dark-black blood into his mouth, and he began to drink from her. Satisfied, she focused again on feeding from him by relaxing her tongue's strong viselike grip, and the smaller barbed fangs relaxed again. She felt the soft suction growing upon her wrist and thought to herself, *It's working!* They were locked together in an unholy embrace, yet more candles sputtered out. Then as if by strange chance, her wrist slipped slightly from his lips for but a moment, and a single stream of black blood ran down her arm. She looked over suddenly and saw it and tried in vain to stop it, but a small drop of jet fell upon the mattress below them. There upon the white sheets was a minuscule splatter

IN THE NAME OF SIN

of jet-black blood that steamed from the enormous heat emanating from it but was rapidly becoming ash.

Then her eyes changed from that of happiness to utter sorrow. She wrenched her wrist away from his mouth. Her long tongue blade shifted slightly and then began to bore deeper while the barbed fangs bored down a squeeze further, embedding the sharp fangs. Then she deeply buried her long fang into his chest, lacerating his heart thoroughly; the man beneath her groaned, and then his back arched in pain. But her body shifted again, and her feeding sped up with such speed as it siphoned the life from his very body and began to drain his very soul! As if by fate, the last of the dying candles sputtered out as darkness closed in around them and more sounds of flesh horribly tearing accompanied it.

Moments later, the scent of burned-out candles and spilled blood filled the room as the large grandfather clock in the corner chimed midnight. Then suddenly a pained wail filled the air followed by a shrieking scream of agony and torment. She fell to her knees from the bed, blood still running down her chest and dribbled from her lips; she grabbed her long black hair and let out yet another sickly moaning scream. Just then, the door to the room burst open, and the bedroom chamber flooded with light. Upon the bed was the corpse of the man she had once been straddling and sharing a tender moment before. The contorted look of terror and confusion was now etched upon his face and the betrayal in his eyes. She looked up slowly from her bloodied hands to the source of light from the doorway as a shadowed figure appeared, once again dimming the light of the room.

"Michelle, what's wrong?" he asked quickly and realized the answer to his question was plainly evident in front of him.

She looked up at him with rage and sorrow in her eyes. "I failed, Elijah… I killed him too… I had to…or I'd be dead also," she said through labored breaths.

Elijah walked slowly toward Michelle and knelt next to her, taking in the macabre scene before him. "You did the only thing you could. These things happen, my young prodigy. Not every attempt at creating is successful. You knew the risks and so did he," he said, pointing at the body on the bed smeared with rapidly coagulating blood.

She looked toward the bed, slowly seeing fully the end result of her failure. Quickly Michelle glared back at Elijah and then let loose a horrid scream that shook the very walls of the room, knocking him backward.

Then Michelle rose inhumanly fast and headed toward the lone door. "I'm going to kill someone or something, Elijah! I'm fucking cursed—that's the only explanation. This is twice now," she screamed back at him, heading toward the door.

But Elijah stood up quickly and grabbed her from behind, pinning her arms behind her back. Michelle's monstrous black claws formed once more from her petite hands in response, but with her arms pinned to her sides, they were worthless. The tussle spilled into the hallway where the bright light, along with the old crimson-painted walls of the hallway, made for an eerie glow that reflected off the well-worn but heavily waxed dark hardwood floors, which creaked in the struggle. Elijah held Michelle tightly as she hissed, and her long tongue lashed and snapped out her mouth. Her hands were hopelessly locked behind her back. But her thoughts were only of vengeance for the moment that was stolen from her, but she fought hard trying to wriggle free. Just then two servants sprinted down the hallway to help restrain her, but another scream from her bloodied lips knocked them away.

Elijah then softly whispered into Michelle's ear softly, "Enough of this, my prodigy, enough, I will not let you go and allow you to leave behind more regret in your wake. Calm now, before I must get stern with you."

The mental command worked, and she ceased struggling as her monstrous claws subsided. Immortals couldn't cry, but all Michelle wanted to do was just that. Her body heaved, yet no tears came from her eyes. Elijah knew what was next but held on to her, as Michelle retched hard, and then her meal from moments before expelled from her mouth in the form a gruesome mess and onto the fine hardwood floors. The scent of putrid essence mixed with bile filled the hallway as Elijah scooped up the now spent Michelle in his arms, and he began walking down the halls past the servants who were still trying to stand.

He glanced down at them roughly but never broke his stride. "Clean up this mess and dispose of the body quickly while I attend to her."

Michelle glanced up from his arms with a crushed look upon her face. "Please be gentle with him…this wasn't his fault…it was mine," she said softly, then her head fell to the side.

Elijah nodded to her but still never broke his stride, nor did he look back at them as they turned on the lights. As the servants entered the room, a small gasp of horror filled the hallway and vanished just as fast in the gloom.

PART 1

CHAPTER 1

October 3, 1991

The cool night air of fall blew through one of the many train stations of Queens, New York. A lone figure stood atop a train trestle waiting for not only the next train to Manhattan but for a friend of his that seemed to be running late as well. Nineteen-year-old Antonio "Tony" Willhiem, to his disdain, had lived in Queens all his life. He was of average height but built quite well due to his time at the martial arts academy near his house. He had been taking lessons there since he was seven and only a few weeks ago got his second-dan black belt in aikido. He had his brown hair trimmed recently and was trying hard to keep his good shirt along with the dress pants he was wearing quite clean. Growing up here, he knew what it could be like sometimes waiting for a train at night on a midweek day in fall—dark, cold, and lonely. Every now and then he looked back seeing if anyone was coming up the escalator or stairs. Between his feet was crumpled brown paper bag that held a six-pack of beer hidden in it. He glanced down at his watch yet again and shook his head, getting annoyed.

"C'mon, Kenny, damn it, I'm not waiting for this next fucking train," Tony said, kneeling down, and took a can of beer out of the bag and opened it.

He took a quick sip of the ice-cold can, trying to keep his hand warm enough to not lose the feeling in it. Taking another fast drink, he settled back, leaning on one of the many billboards lining the platform, and shook his head. He was just about to take another drink when someone called out from the dark stairwell.

"Hey, Willhiem, if you're gonna drink all the beer, you're buying more, you damn lush!" a voice called out from his side that he had known for quite a while.

But Tony spit out the beer in his mouth after being startled and saw someone he had been waiting for finally walking up the back stairs. Once he got closer, he nearly threw his can at him.

"Damn it, Kenny, anyone ever tell you you're a fucking asshole?" he replied, taking another can out of the bag and tossing it to him.

"Thank you, and to answer your question, umm, yeah, you every day when we got brave enough to curse out loud," Kenny said back, laughing, and zipped up his beat-up leather jacket then brushed his long hair out of his face.

He leaned back on the billboard with Tony and took out a cigarette along with his Zippo and lit it before the next gust of wind whipped through the station. With a snap he opened the can of beer and downed it in three gulps, tossing the can to the dirty tracks below. Tony just took another small drink from his can, and Kenny asked him for another one. He tossed it to him, and he opened that one too and took a big drink from the can.

"Kenny, man, slow down, at the rate you're going, you could kill a case of these. Sooner or later, that'll kill ya," Tony said to him quickly, but Kenny took another big gulp and took a big drag from his cigarette also.

"So will smoking, but who's counting, and more importantly, who gives a shit either?" Kenny replied to him with a wry grin.

Tony had to laugh out loud and tossed him another beer. They had been best friends forever, total polar opposites throughout school. Where Tony was always into martial arts and cared about his grades while trying to maybe get into college. Your basically good kid that drifted through high school most times unnoticed. Kenny was a total rebel that didn't care much about school at all, ditched often,

IN THE NAME OF SIN

and barely graduated, thanks to Tony's help. His only love was music; Kenny played guitar and owned about five, and he was really good. He was in a few bands throughout school and dreamed of getting big in the rock and metal genre. He had the skills, but all he needed was a damn chance. Tony shook his head while thinking for a moment and was the first to ask after he drained his own can, tossing it to the tracks.

"Where were you, and I wasn't waiting for the next train, man," he said, still watching him take another huge drink from the can of beer.

Kenny then took another drag of his cigarette and then slowed down on his beer finally. "That asshole McLeod had me stay late because of some bullshit in the back that you'd know about if you showed up for work today. That new guy is an idiot, by the way— how do you fuck up loading boxes? Put boxes on the boat and wheel it out, not hard, right? But no, this dude can't get that done, so who's gotta fix it? Yours truly, that's who. Fucking assholes, both of 'em. I should've quit," he said, taking another drag of his cigarette and then a drink.

"Hey, you know I took off today to teach at the academy again, or I would've helped ya. We've got that tournament coming up, and we need to place well so we can get some publicity for the academy. God knows they need it," Tony said, grabbing another beer and cracking it open, taking a sip.

"Yeah, yeah, I know, but still, if you had been there, I wouldn't have been stuck with a mental midget. I probably would've gotten home with enough time to take a damn shower instead of just changing clothes. Still, who cares, wait till you see this place in Chelsea, man. It's off the hook. You brought the fake ID I helped you get, right?" Kenny asked, finally smiling and taking a drag of his cigarette.

Tony then looked back at him and pointed down at the bag as he took another sip off his can. Kenny nodded and looked down the tracks and thought he saw lights in the distance. "Train, Willhiem, you better finish that brew. You know how much the conductors love open containers on the train, right?"

Tony looked down the tracks and saw lights in the distance going west toward the city. "Here, take it. I can finish one that fast!"

But Kenny looked over at him and laughed. "I'm not drinking your backwash brew, you bitch, you opened it, now chug that beer, you pussy!"

Tony dented the front of the can right near the opening and hated this. He started drinking fast; if he spilled on his jacket or shirt, he was going to punch Kenny. He drank fast, and Kenny laughed at him again.

"CHUG THAT!" he yelled at him as the lights got closer, and the horn blared.

Tony finished it and tossed the can down to the tracks and snatched up the bag. "You're an asshole, you know that," he said as the train pulled in fast with a screech.

"So, I've been told," Kenny said, looking back with a smirk.

Once they got on the train, they found a few empty seats at the back of the car and sat across from each other, keeping an eye out for the conductors. Kenny looked over at him, and Tony tossed him one of the last cans. He slid it into his pocket and then glanced back over at him.

"Hey, genius, you need a ticket to ride this thing. You got one, right?" Kenny asked him with another smirk on his face.

Tony cursed a little too loud and shook his head, because his mind had been other places lately. He was still finishing his college applications, and his mother was on his back to get them done daily. His friend Chuck was home for the upcoming holidays; he had taught him some martial arts to help him as an offensive lineman, and he turned his play around so well he had a full ride to school. Chuck's steady girlfriend since high school, Liz, was attending another school about thirty minutes away on a soccer and lacrosse scholarship, so that had worked out well for them both. But in the summer, Tony's steady girlfriend throughout most of high school had broken up with him just before she moved to school. Ashley thought it was best to take some time off from each other instead of a long-distance relationship from her dorm. After that, it seemed like his black cloud of bad luck had returned. He missed the Olympic team tryout by two damn points in his last competition, but he got picked for the alternate team; still, that didn't mean much either. Then an injury to his knee during training all but removed him from the alternate team. Now he was trying to get into college, and it was a constant stream of rejection letters lately. Things couldn't get much worse, he thought; he had a lousy job, at almost nineteen, and he felt like he was wasting his life away in Queens, like his father did before he vanished.

He then looked over at Kenny again and sighed. "I guess I'll buy it on the train," he said back dejectedly.

But then Kenny handed him a ticket. "For the beer. And you gotta snap out of it. Besides, Ashley was a bitch," he said, and Tony nodded to him but was still a little upset.

They both saw the conductor soon making his way steadily toward them, and Kenny stashed the beer he was just about to open. Still Tony needed a decent night these days; he was hoping his blind date tonight would go well. He hadn't told Kenny about that yet, that they were meeting Chuck, Liz, and their friend Brittney at the nightclub. Hopefully he wouldn't be too pissed off, but hey, he had to try to find something good in his life maybe.

CHAPTER 2

Meanwhile, inside a dark apartment in Gramercy, Manhattan, Michelle Du'Pree woke up and took in the scent of blood around her for her first aroma of the night. She sat up slowly, and her silky raven locks bounced once as she glanced around the room for the source of that familiar scent. She then saw what she was looking for on the floor over to the right, a severed human arm. She placed her bare feet on the floor and stepped over the dismembered arm, heading to the small bathroom. She flipped on the light and cursed once. She was covered in blood from the obvious arterial spray from probably severing the limb on the floor. Damn it, she was going to have to go home first before heading to the club, she thought to herself. She shook her head and turned on the water, trying to wash her face at least.

Then the night came back to her fully, and she hung her head. Her latest boy toy was wreck in the other room obviously. Why couldn't Jimmy, a good-looking investment banker on Wall Street, just have a bit of fun? Why did he have to say that last night? Then pushed the issue with his obvious lies. She took a step back into the apartment, and the classically decorated New York apartment was showered with blood. The macabre scene in front of her was the beautiful cream-colored walls had blood everywhere, and the dark hardwood floors and accents held countless more splatters. She had slipped last night and gave in to her unnatural thirsts, and the result was total carnage. Michelle was an Immortal, a kind of half human, half demon more commonly known as Succubus, but she lived forever and had terrible demonic powers. Unlike fabled vampires, she was very much alive, enjoyed parties and everything else human beings did, just like food and drink, and especially sex—damn, a Succubus absolutely loved sex! This was due to her elevated libido or being a temptation or lust demoness. But her other side, the demonic one, had to feed too; and in order to do that, she needed human life force found in the fresh bloodstream of her victim. It wasn't blood at all she was looking for, like a classic vampire though, hence why there was a lot of it everywhere. It was the life force or—what her kind called it—*essence* hidden inside it, and it was where the soul swam. Most times Immortals took just a little, but last night looked pretty bad though.

Michelle walked through the apartment and found her blouse and jacket still dripping with blood. She walked past it and found one of her boots, and next to it, she found most of what was left of Jimmy. He was a very good-looking, well-built, and tan thirty-something she had met at the club a few nights ago. Yes, it looked like she was dating an older man, but in fact, Michelle was going on two hundred and seventy-five years old. She flipped the body over, and his eyes were stark white, and she cursed again. She had drained his soul because the eyes were windows to the soul, and he didn't have any, not anymore at least. Michelle hung her head and now remembered how this started. Why did Jimmy say those three little words that they both knew meant nothing? He just wanted her for what she had: Michelle Du'Pree, the heiress, the socialite, club brat, the millionairess, and from a prominent Manhattan family. Not for the reasons they should ever be spoken. If he had just kept that lie to himself, he'd be alive this evening. Michelle would've fed a little and made sure the sex they had was the absolute best in his life, and that would have been that. But no, he had to say, "I love you," when they both knew he didn't mean it at all!

She flipped the mangled body over again, so it was facedown once more. She didn't want to see those empty, lifeless eyes anymore; they disturbed her. She then started to look for his shirt because he had obviously taken it off first. She just hoped it didn't have too much blood on it. Immortals being demons were very good at killing; the problem was being this good at it usually left a huge mess behind. Michelle found his shirt on the couch, and it was clean enough, so she covered her chest and her beautiful rose tattoo on her back then began to head for a phone in the place. This apartment was going to need to be cleaned thoroughly, and luckily, she knew the right people to call, her family. She still had to get cleaned up and get to the club on time, so she had a solid alibi about being home when this happened. But she didn't feel like showering in a damn crime scene either! She picked up the phone and dialed, and it rang twice. Someone finally picked up, and Michelle spoke for the first time tonight but had to clear her throat first. As she did, she felt her tongue split slightly, and then she spoke.

"Elijah, yeah, I had a little accident over in Gramercy, and I fucked up," she said, annoyed; as she waited for him to say something, she took in the scene, and all she could think was, How the fuck did she sleep in here?

Meanwhile, Penn Station was nothing special for either Tony or Kenny, but they had to hurry to catch the next subway to Chelsea to get to the club Kenny was talking about. They walked down the stairs of the station and made the subway with a few minutes to spare. Kenny had finished his last beer on the train, but Tony tossed him the last one he had in his jacket pocket. He caught it and tapped the lid of the can twice and pulled the tab.

"Whatever I've said about you in the past, Willhiem, forget it, you're the man," he said and took a long drink from the can.

But he said nothing back and hoped a simple can of beer would be enough to smooth over the next thing he was going to tell Kenny. As the subway pulled up and stopped, they both got in and found a few seats but checked them before they sat. Next, Tony turned toward Kenny, who had just taken the last pull of the beer and ditched the can on the floor in case one of New York's finest was on the train tonight too.

"Okay, you've been quiet the whole time we got in this subway car and gave me the last beer. What's going on, Tony, you look like you're going to ask me something, and you know I hate that," he said with a quick joke, but Tony decided just to tell him.

"We're meeting Chuck and Liz at the club, and I'm on a blind date tonight too," he blurted out, and Kenny gave him a shocked look that made him feel horrible at the moment.

"Oh, for fuck's sake! Is there a way off this thing, like, now! Why would you do that? Wait till you see this place. It's not the joint you bring a date to, let alone a blind date. I mean those two are one thing, but seriously. I brought you here to unwind and maybe get you laid, but you brought a few people along. That should wreck this plan—good job, man," Kenny said back, visibly upset.

Kenny and Chuck didn't get along and throughout school were part of two opposing cliques. Chuck was on the football team, and Kenny was a rebel and always in trouble. They never hung out together; now Tony had thrown them together and was forceable too.

"Look, he was home from school and wanted to stop by tonight, so I told him not tonight, and he got the plans out of me. So, I thought why not, high school is over, we can get along, right?" Tony said back, trying his best to convince him.

Kenny looked back at him and could never stay angry at him for long, ever since they were kids. He was always the negotiator even though Tony could fight better than anyone in school. He had learned a mixed form of aikido, but he was always the first one to try to use words to stop a conflict. Kenny looked right at him and finally nodded with a weak smile; he hated this, but what were they supposed to do?

"Yeah, I guess, you did buy the beer, but why, why the damn blind date, jeez," he asked, shaking his head and slowly looking down.

The two of them then laughed out loud and had a few jokes about it, but still they were supposed to be heading to one of the most popular places in New York City's nightlife right now.

Back in SoHo, Michelle Du'Pree walked into her flat look-ing disheveled from the night before. She couldn't believe how eas-ily blood got all over you when you're that angry. The apartment would be cleaned, and her alibi would be set as long as she arrived at the Factory in Chelsea in less than hour. She walked up the three stairs of her flat and then suddenly moved like a blur, setting up the coffeepot first. Within seconds, coffee was brewing, thankfully. Next, she rocketed down the hallway and ran through the shower, and within moments, she was clean and had her hair in a towel. She raced into her closet and took out a few things and tossed them on the bed. Then as if she never moved at all, she reappeared with cup of black coffee and upended the mug, setting it on her nightstand. She walked over and looked into the mirror and let her hair down and then rapidly shook her head, and when she was done, her hair was dry but a mess. Michelle then sat down at her vanity and began to do her hair and makeup. Within a short blur, she looked like herself, and she picked up her clothes and rapidly got dressed, and she was ready for the night. She shut the lights to her room and walked over to a dark corner and vanished, only to reappear in the kitchen. Michelle grabbed the hot coffeepot and took a long drink, realizing afterward she'd have to touch her face up in the car for that. She was heading for the front door, but the phone rang. Breathing out hard and annoyed, she picked it up reluctantly.

"Yes, what is it?" she asked, annoyed and trying to leave because the earlier she arrived, the better this looked. She was grabbing her favorite jacket when Elijah finally answered.

"Tell me you're ready to go?" he said in an annoyed tone of his own.

"Of course, I am, it's not like I haven't done this before," she answered, looking into a mirror on the wall and fixing her hair with her fingers.

"Michelle, what the blazes happened to your latest boy toy? He was in pieces, and that apartment, it's wrecked too. You do know you drained him, right? What could possibly warrant that, so tell me, what happened?" Elijah asked in an angry tone now.

Michelle looked out the window and saw the limousine pulling up and grabbed her bag. "Me, I did, Elijah, that's what happened, ME," she said back and hung up the phone roughly.

She then walked out the front door in less than fifteen minutes; no mortal woman could look this good in that little time, she thought as she got into the car, alibi set.

*****

The autumn night of New York City had a bit of light rain in the air. It was slowly wetting the sidewalk outside the Factory. Tony and Kenny were on the line waiting to get in, and Kenny hated that it wasn't just Tony and him, but he was dealing with it. Just then, from behind, Chuck and Liz showed up with her friend Brittney from school. It didn't help that Tony had an impromptu blind date that he had kept from Kenny until the subway ride here. They all settled into the line, and it was moving slowly to the front doors. All of them were hoping to get in because this place filled up fast even on the weekdays, and it wasn't looking good right now either. Kenny started to complain that they should have arrived even earlier.

The Factory was unlike any nightclub, if you could call it that, in the city. On the outside, it looked just like what it was called, an old turn-of-the-century factory. On the inside, it was a four-level nightclub completely devoted to entertainment in the city. This was the celebrities' or socialites' first choice in the entire island of Manhattan. The first level was a posh bar that served nothing but the very best drinks and liquor around. It was treated more of a meeting point and happened to be connected to what looked like the lobby of a five-star hotel as people entered. White marble, deep oak trims, crystal chandeliers—the works. The second floor was your basic nightclub setting—dancing, hanging out, DJs, bottle service, and huge VIP sections. The third floor was an all-night rave in the darkness of the room that started when the club opened, and stopped when it closed—no rules and really no one watching too. Some people said it was almost too easy to get drugs on the third floor. The fourth floor was a concert hall for live entertainment, complete with private sky booths and only open when it was booked, which was often by huge bands looking for an intimate setting for their fans. The club was situated in an open avenue, and the paparazzi weren't even allowed to approach the club; that's why it had become so popular with socialites and celebrities. If someone from the paparazzi even set foot on this side of the avenue the Factory was on, they were arrested. The best they could do was stand across from it and use what telephoto lenses they had. Even cameras were strictly forbidden inside the Factory; if you were caught with one, you'd be tossed, and the policy of the club was once you were thrown out, you never came back. Then came what made the place legendary: below was the famed Abyss, the club inside a club. No one knew anything about it, but rumors had it, it was strictly invitation only. Most people who came here hoped to get the invite, and no one knew how to get one, and the members weren't talking either. Even famous celebrities had been turned away from the black velvet ropes blocking the huge stairway down. The cover charge was steep to get in, two drinks minimum were enforced, and it was either getset here early or sit on the lines that sometimes stretched four city blocks. That's where they were all hoping to spend the evening together, and now it felt like you had to be lucky to get in too.

So now they all waited in line patiently, and as they got near the front, a long black limousine pulled up at the curb. Two people came down to open the door, and out stepped what Tony thought was the most beautiful and sexy girl he had ever seen in his life! Her long silky raven-black hair gently blew in the autumn wind; her skin looked so flawless, it was like perfect alabaster; her lips were a perfect shade of red; and her deep blue eyes sparkled in the moonlight that she quickly hid behind her dark glasses. Tony couldn't help it; he looked her up and down and was drawn in with ease and swallowed hard just trying not to stare. In his mind, she was a total knockout! Her body was the perfect mix of a supermodel and movie star, but she had something that put her above even those standards. Her perfect face was like that of old Hollywood beauty that women today paid thousands for and never came close. As she strutted slowly toward the door, her hips swayed so sexily, and you could hear the clacking of her knee-high, long stiletto-heeled boots on the ground. As she got closer, Tony turned away before she noticed him checking her out.

Meanwhile, Michelle had noticed the boy behind the ropes was watching her, and she had his attention entirely. He was quite handsome in a simple way, which she liked. He had a good physique, and she could tell he obviously worked out in some way to keep it like that. He was wearing plain black pants, a crisp button-up shirt, along with a faded leather jacket. She began to walk past and lowered her glasses to look right at him, but he had turned away, not wanting to embarrass himself. *How cute*, she thought. It was then she watched something that nearly floored her though. The rain was starting to pick up a bit, and the girl next to him was underdressed, to say the least, for fall. But the boy took off his jacket and draped it around her shoulders to shield her from the rain and cold. Michelle's mouth opened a little in shock, but she recovered fast. She hadn't seen chivalry like that in such long time, and that got her attention fully. As she walked past the bouncer, she made sure he was getting in tonight so she could see what else he had to surprise her with.

From the doors, she looked back, and then their eyes met for just a moment. This time Michelle turned away fast, and her heart fluttered for a second, but she continued on. Meanwhile, Tony had seen her look back quickly, and it looked like she was checking him out! Kenny was the first to notice it too and then nudged Tony.

"Hey, bro, that's one of the club's regulars, one of the VIPs, and I think she was looking right at ya! You lucky bastard!" he said, and Tony just shook his head.

"No way she could possibly care about me. Besides, I'm here with someone tonight," he said to Brittney with a smile.

Confidently, Tony took her hand as they walked up the stairs and into the club. But in the back of his mind, he swore she was looking right at him too. But he thought that couldn't be right, could it? There was no way a girl of that caliber would even consider him.

CHAPTER 3

Up on the third floor of the Factory, Tony sat and watched as a few of his friends were enjoying the show and dancing. He had all but forgotten about the girl before, but Tony didn't dance at all and had not wanted to embarrass himself at one of the city's most premier clubs either. He watched on as Kenny got yet another beer from the bar, and he had lost sight of Chuck and Liz for the moment; meanwhile, Brittney was dancing with close to three guys now. What he didn't notice was that he was being watched too. From the shadows, Michelle Du'Pree had finally found her mystery man from outside. It was the boy that had gotten her attention at the front doors before. The very one that she had told the bouncers to let in, his friends included, just so she could maybe run into him. She slowly moved to the left and sat down watching and thinking and wore a sly grin on her lips. She was deciding if he was worth the effort to meet him or not, but still, she was very intrigued. The song at the rave was speeding up, and Michelle noticed he wasn't dancing out on the floor like she hoped, but the girl he came with was. She now saw this as open season, and this was her club. Not to mention what she wanted usually became hers anyway. There was no reason that this interesting human should be any different in her eyes. She then got up and moved a bit closer in the darkness and unnoticed, and then she vanished into the crowd.

IN THE NAME OF SIN

At the table, Tony let out another laugh as Chuck almost fell dancing with Liz, and he had lost sight of Brittney completely now. Just then the chair next to him slid out, and someone slipped right into it quickly. He slowly looked over, and it was the girl from the front of the club! She smiled widely and set down her finished drink on the table.

"So, tell me, do you still like what you see?" she asked in a very sexy voice.

Tony was absolutely embarrassed right now, and she had obviously seen him looking. "I'm sorry, I didn't mean to upset you or disrespect you in any way," he stammered, trying to not check her out again because she was stunning, and he was failing miserably.

After a brief moment of silence from her, she began to laugh so loudly, and Tony was a bit confused. She put her hands over her mouth trying to stop laughing after another moment.

"Oh my god, you should see your face right now! Why do you think I dress this way and come to nightclubs? I was quite flattered, you know," she said back with a sexy grin on her lips.

Tony let out a sigh of relief and introduced himself to her. Then she looked out to the dance floor and began to stand up. She put out her hand, but he shook his head back.

"I don't dance, I'm sorry," he said.

But she began to pout with her deep-red lips and took his hand anyway. She pulled him to his feet and led him to the dance floor with hardly any coaxing.

"You do now," she said and took the lead.

The song slowed a bit, and Michelle took it easy on him; just then the energy shifted, and for that moment and in his arms, everything felt so right to her. It's like she belonged here, her heart felt it! Then her sensitive Immortal skin had felt the static-like energy when she took his hand, surging through her fingertips, soothing her. Could he be...but then she shook off the idea. She continued to dance with him through quite a few songs, and when the music slowed down again, she found her head felt absolutely right on his chest. Michelle looked up at his nervous face and smiled back, trying to soothe him now.

"You're doing fine, just enjoy me and my company," she purred to him.

Then she felt him begin to loosen up, and Michelle led him toward the bar. With a tap of her finger as they danced past on the bar, the bartender began to fix her a drink. After yet another song in which Tony felt much more relaxed throughout, she stopped and took his hand in hers.

"Let's have a drink you and I, you've gotta be thirsty, I know I am," she said with a small wink.

When they returned to the bar, Michelle's Crown and Cola was waiting with a beer for him. They picked up their drinks, and she took his hand again. She then led him to a dark table near the back of the room and sat close with him.

"Who said you couldn't dance? You did fine, you know," she said, leaning back and relaxing, showing off her body.

Tony took a long drink off his bottle and let out a sigh of relief. "I was so worried I was going to embarrass you," he answered, and she let out another laugh.

"Of course not, you did fine, and I found you refreshing. You got better with time, you know," she said, putting her hand on his and smiling widely.

After a bit of chitchat, she then took his hand again after she finished her drink. "You know, there's live music up on the fourth floor, let's go. You look good on me tonight," she said and began to stand up, and her eyes just looked right into his for a moment.

"Oh, I don't have a ticket to get in there," he said back to her, but she still took his hand, and this time he felt that static shock surge through his hand.

"Nonsense, you're with me now, you can go anywhere I go, I'm your little ticket tonight," Michelle said to him in a sexy voice. Just as they had walked to the stairs that took them up, Tony ran right into Chuck, Liz, and Brittney.

"There you are, and where ya going, man?" Chuck asked him, realizing he was heading for the stairs.

Michelle took a step forward and was now annoyed. She never liked it when something got in the way of a supposed interest of hers or a possible meal.

"With me," she said with a slight frown, seeing her plans had been interrupted.

Hearing that, Brittney then decided to take a step forward. "He's with me tonight, you know?"

Michelle looked back at Tony and then to Brittney and grinned a little. "I never saw your label on him. He was sitting there all alone while you danced with not one, but three different men, and I saw him as fair game. You know how it goes—finders keepers."

Brittney and Liz then got mad, but Michelle took Tony's hand again and motioned to go up. He turned and then let go of her hand reluctantly, but Michelle knew he wanted to go with her.

"I did come here with her. It isn't right, but thank you, I had a great time," Tony said, still trying to not look silly.

Then Brittney grinned and shouted at her, "Hit the road, bitch!"

Michelle, now annoyed, took a step off the stairs and glared right at her, and Brittney's smirk faded slowly. "You're lucky I like him, skank, or you'd all be leaving here the hard way," Michelle said, and her deep blue eyes seemed to blaze for a just a moment.

She then turned to Tony and took his hand again but let go as she got to the stairs, never looking away from his eyes. She left behind two stunned women and two infatuated men in her wake, and Michelle loved it. She enjoyed it when women hated her and men just desired her.

"When you lose that," she said pointing to Brittney from over her shoulder, "come and find me here. I'll be waiting for you, cutie," she purred and then kissed him right on the lips and then caressed his cheek with the back of her hand, leaving him stunned as she headed up the stairs.

Tony shook his head, shaking off the shock of being kissed suddenly by a woman he thought was the most beautiful he had ever seen. He watched her strutting up the stairs from below, then he realized something.

"I didn't get your name!" he said to her and nearly stammered getting that out.

She looked down once more and winked again. "I didn't give it, come and find me here though. I'll be waiting. Maybe you can get my name next time. Bye-bye, sexy," she said back, blowing him yet another kiss, and then vanished to the floor above.

All of them were exasperated with what just happened merely moments ago. When they headed back to the table, both Brittney and Liz were furious, but Chuck was oddly silent still. Only Tony kept looking at the stairs wanting to go find her again. What he didn't know was that a subtle mental command was given when she left. And not one of them noticed Michelle watching him from a distance the rest of the night too from time to time. Once again, she was impressed; he refused her since he was with someone. This one was quite special after all, she thought. If he wouldn't leave that little tart for her, then imagine how he'd be when he did belong to her, she thought silently and grinned. She liked Tony and hoped he would come back very soon and felt he would. He kept looking back at the stairs for hours; she had him wrapped around her little finger, Michelle thought to herself in the shadows of the third floor.

Later in the night and on the train ride back to Queens, both the girls were still furious with that "little bitch" from the club, as they called her. They kept talking about her and saying, "Who is she to act like that!" Chuck had a look of disgust on his face—not from that, but that every conversation seemed to revolve around that incident. It was Kenny who kept saying quietly to Tony that he had to get back to the club because the girl was beyond hot. But it was Tony who kept quiet on the train and who was still in shock from tonight's turn of events. What he hadn't told any of them was he couldn't get her out of his head. He still felt her sensual touch and smell her sweet perfume that seemed to be stuck on his clothes. He couldn't believe that he had danced with a girl that looked like that; she was so alluring! Still, it seemed wrong to just go to the fourth floor with her and leave them on the floor below. He had also agreed to the blind date tonight too. But as much as he kept rationalizing it, he couldn't shake her from his mind, but he didn't even know her name. Kenny kept chatting it up with him thinking this was the greatest night of his life, but Tony wasn't too sure. There was something about her that was a little off; still, he was so smitten and secretly wanted to get back to the Factory as soon as he could. It was almost like he needed to get back to her as soon as he could, but why?

CHAPTER 4

The very next night, Tony got moving early and was heading to Manhattan again—this time alone. It was like something was guiding him—no, calling to him, and he had to know who she was. It was like something was demanding he had to know her name. The train pulled into the station, and he stepped inside, taking the rickety ride toward the city. But Tony swore he could still smell her distinct perfume that seemed to only get stronger as the train pulled into Penn Station. Tony had never had a girl get into his head like she had. All day he kept seeing her in different places—in the neighborhood and at his job too. He couldn't concentrate on anything; even when teaching aikido today to the younger kids, he kept getting distracted. He then rubbed his jaw where a student had hit him because he wasn't paying enough attention. Tony walked out into the station and then began to head to the subway trains that would take him to Chelsea. As he walked up from the station, he saw a news vendor that had fresh flowers. He checked the money in his pocket and figured he had enough to bring her a few, if he even found her. Tony was so surprised how fresh the roses were and bought half a dozen at a pretty good price. As he watched the vendor wrap them, the man asked him who was the girl getting these. Tony took the bouquet and looked up, lost in thought from another moment yet again. He said back to the vendor that he didn't even know her name. The man nodded

IN THE NAME OF SIN

and finished wrapping the roses and handed them to him. He then turned and walked down to the next station, and the eerie lights of night in the city reminded him not to get too lost in thought while he was here alone. He walked down to the station and got to the train platform just in time as the subway train pulled in. Tony then stepped inside, and the doors closed behind him; in a few stops, he'd be in Chelsea.

Meanwhile in her SoHo flat, Michelle had gotten up at the same time as every night she had for fifty-two years. She stretched a bit and let out a slow yawn, shaking off the day's sleep. She could never figure out how after two hundred and seventy-five years she still woke up groggy though. She then stood and headed for the en suite to get ready for her night at the club and her guest, who should already be there when she arrived too. Dancing with him last night made her realize that this was no quick meal and done. She liked him and meant to find out why too. She had felt the electricity in the air while they danced, and whatever that was, she couldn't just let it go or get it out of her head. She was a Succubus after all; when they got interested, it was for very good reasons too, and something had struck her fancy. When that happened, it was rare, and now she was very interested indeed.

After a quick shower and then doing her makeup, which was very similar to last night's, she walked over to her massive closet and walked inside. She ran her hand down the well-organized rows of freshly cleaned clothes. She then began to wonder how to dress because she had gotten his attention so easily last night in her knee-high leather boots, tight black pants, white silk blouse, and her faded motorcycle jacket that was actually from the '50s. She then realized she needed to head out and go shopping one night soon because she didn't have anything to wear; a call to her girls was in order. She continued to look, and she was trying to decide between classy or slutty. She then decided on a pink silk top with a short black miniskirt. She then spied the tan box on top of the shoe rack. She pulled it down, and her brand-new custom calf-length shorter-heeled stilettos were inside. They were delivered last month, and she had forgotten all about them. She then found a pair of fishnet stockings to go with them. Finally, her new hip-length leather jacket to finish off this ensemble. Michelle decided to change her hair and let her raven locks flow like last night. She looked herself over in the closet mirror and then decided on her earrings for the night. A little retro '80s with this outfit seemed to fit, so she took out a pair of large gold hoops. She looked again and was content; her tattoo on her back showed just a little through the blouse. She began to walk out of the closet and laughed to herself; if she got his attention last night that easy, she was going to blow his mind tonight. Michelle then looked to the clock on the wall and realized she was going to be fifteen minutes late getting to the club. She blew it off as being fashionably late, and it took some time to look this fabulous. She then walked out of her flat toward the waiting black limousine outside.

Back in Chelsea, Tony had arrived early enough, and the line was still long again. He was starting to feel stupid now because how was he supposed to find one girl in a place like this among so many people? He didn't even know her name; he had just been let in a little while ago, but strangely no cover charges, but he never even saw her limo pull up. He decided to go back to the third floor and to the same set of tables and chairs as last night in hopes they would just run into each other again. He was also hoping she didn't think he was an idiot too. He had come back looking for her not knowing her name after just dancing and sharing one drink. Yes, she had kissed him, but he was starting to think she did that to just piss off his date. He continued to look out into the crowd, but he was starting to think it was time to go, that she wasn't going to come here again. He had his chance last night—and blew it when he didn't go up to fourth floor with her. He was about to get up when the seat slid out next to him and someone slipped right into it quickly. He looked over slowly, and it was her! She took her dark glasses off, and her deep blue eyes met his once more.

"You came back for little ole me, I didn't think you would, you were pretty adamant about that other little bitch last night," she lied, knowing full well he would be here.

Tony tried to speak, but she was even more gorgeous than she was last night. She was mesmerizing, like something swirled around

IN THE NAME OF SIN

her drawing him to her. Tony then smelled her perfume again, and it nearly hazed his mind too. Meanwhile, Michelle found it very cute in her eyes because she knew she had him now. She had been subtly letting lust swirl around the room when she sat down and surprised him again.

"I hope no friends tonight because I'd like you all to myself this time." She then spied the flowers he was holding and grinned widely. "Ah, are those for me? How thoughtful," she said and reached for the roses.

Tony pulled them away a bit playfully though. "They might be for you, but first, you've gotta tell me your name so I know who I'm giving them to."

Michelle liked him before; now she really liked him because he had refused her twice, but in her mind, he wasn't getting a third. "My, my, aren't we adamant and inventive. Well, if you must know, I'm Michelle, Michelle Victoria Du'Pree."

Tony handed her the flowers, and their fingers touched, and both of them felt that same electricity from last night—this time at the same time. Then he sat back for a bit and thought for a moment.

"Du'Pree, I know that name for some reason. Why can't I place it right now?" he said, still watching her take a deep breath smelling the fresh cut roses.

"Oh, you've probably heard of my mother, Anneke Elizabeth Du'Pree. She's the talk of the social circles in the city lately…again," she said back, taking in the sweet aroma of the roses once more and then setting them on table.

But how could he possibly have known they were her absolu favorites, deep-crimson roses, she thought once more, taking in th sweet aroma she loved so much. She could see Tony was an aver guy, but he had taken the time to buy her roses without even kn ing her name. He took a chance, too, coming back. *Could th be…* Then she shook her head again, chasing the thoughts away more. But as she was thinking that, Tony's eyes widened sudd he did know the name!

"You're telling me your mother just brokered that deal city for a beautification program in which her companies a most of the contract work? I read about that in the papers last week, that's your mom. Anneke Du'Pree, who the papers call the Queen of New York?" Tony said back, now utterly shocked.

Michelle then blew a lock of errant hair out of her face hearing her name. "Yes, but did you come to talk about my mother, or did you come here for me?" she asked back, now visibly a little annoyed too.

Tony then smiled back to her and looked in her eyes once more. "Definitely you," he said back with a smile.

She then got up, and like last time, she held out her hand, and he took it quickly as they walked out onto the dance floor together. He seemed to be a little more confident this time, and once more, Michelle liked that.

Hours later, the two of them sat together on a comfortable couch on the second-floor VIP area. Michelle had a constant stream of drinks being brought as they began to run out. Tony was starting think he was a bit buzzed but hardly cared. She was sitting with and other guys could only just stand there and watch because as actually interested in him. Michelle sat next to him now g at the back of the room, and it felt like a perfect night for of them. Her boots were casually lying across Tony's knees tted away, laughing from time to time and having a great —his first in a long time. Michelle, on the other hand, ning her lust subtly and throughout the night to keep but like he needed that. It was more to keep others time; she wanted him alone with her. She really liked the constant flow of alcohol and her influence, he h about himself. But surprisingly she was telling ut herself too—of course, leaving out a few key long that Michelle could let her guard down ne. It was like he only cared about her and more. She really liked this one because he y or her family name and all the pres- er round of drinks was served, and he ipped hers; she wasn't letting him get t this. She then realized she needed to stop too because she felt a little tipsy herself, surprisingly. Michelle then smiled widely, taking his hand again; it had been so long since she just had a few drinks with a friend, and this was so special to her. When she finally looked at her watch, she couldn't believe the time! It was two hours to dawn, and they had closed the club down in the same love seat they had been in since dancing before. Soon the bartenders were making the last call, then she had a great idea just then.

"Get up, they're going to close soon. We need to get to the fourth floor," she said, taking her feet off his knee.

"Why, what's on the fourth floor, isn't it closed tonight?" he asked, getting up as she did.

"Yes, and that's the point, silly. Just go with this. You won't be sorry, I promise," she said back, heading for the stairs, his hand in hers.

Together they made their way to the back elevator instead, and Michelle used her key to take them to the fourth floor. Once outside the elevator, she quickly took his hand and walked to the windows that overlooked the city skyline. She then had him stand right next to her.

"Wait for it! Any second now," she said, taking his hand.

The last song from the rave below started, and the floor began vibrating under their feet. She then turned and looked right into his eyes. And they began to sway slowly from the pulsing music below them.

"Now dance with me, it's the last dance, and we're all by ourselves, so take your time," she said, looking over at him seductively with a sexy grin on her lips.

He took her hand, and this time, he led. The dark shades began to descend to close off the widows, but they danced on. As the last light began to fade, Michelle put her hand gently behind his head and gazed into his eyes. She felt his hands wrap around her waist, and it felt perfect, so perfect. They stopped, and within a moment, their lips met; and to her, it felt like liquid fire ignited around the room! Together they shared a very passionate kiss as the shades closed and darkness enveloped them while the music slowly stopped below. Michelle thought it was so romantic, and Tony at that point realized he was falling hard for her, but he had to try to keep his head. Michelle, on the other hand, had practically let lust surge through the room due to that kiss. As they finished their passionate kiss, her tongue split a little in anticipation; she felt he would make a fine meal for her now, after the sexual ideas she had going through her mind at the moment.

Later on as the club closed, Michelle kissed him once more, and then she finally let go of his hand. Even though she was a little upset, she knew he was having a hard time right now letting her go too. As much as she wanted him, he had to be thinking the same thing as well. Still as hard as Michelle was trying to, to tempt him to her bed, Tony was resisting just as much.

"Tomorrow night, you and I, here, and don't make me wait either. You've seen my sweet side, I think you'd like to avoid me getting bratty," she said with a smile and running her fingers through his hair.

Tony didn't want to go, but he had to; she had invited him twice back to her place, and he had said no, and it was tough. All he could think about was her, and as turned on as he was, he found he just couldn't. He didn't want to ruin this moment like that.

"I think I'm working tomorrow night, so I'll try," he said back, trying to convince himself.

She then stepped closer to him, taking his hands once more. "Work or me? I think you should make the right choice here. But that's up to you, but I'd choose me. So, call in sick, and I'll see you at nine, you're on my list for the club. I promise you won't be disappointed, have you been yet?" she said back with a grin and the attitude that made her so unique.

But Tony couldn't take his eyes off her, and Michelle kissed him once more then let go of his hands again. She then headed to her waiting car but looked back for a moment. She knew she had him wrapped around her little finger completely and he'd be here tomorrow. Still, he refused her again when she wanted him to go home with her. The sheer amount of lust in that room should have reduced him to her plaything. If he had said yes, she would have made love to him sweetly, fed, and then took her leave of him. But this one was special indeed, and she was keeping this one for a while at least. Michelle then sat back in her limo and suddenly realized she had made a friend, her first new friend in a decade. She shut the door and watched him head for the subway station. This time she hoped to see him tomorrow because she hadn't used a mental suggestion, but she needed to see if he came to her without it. If he was here tomorrow night, he belonged to her, and she loved the idea of that. Strangely she cared and hoped he got home safely too.

As Tony walked away, he glanced back briefly and called himself an idiot again. She wanted him to go home with her, and he had said no, twice! After the way their date had ended, he thought he had to be completely out of his mind. He had to figure out how to get out of work. He liked her, he really liked her. But how could a girl with money and notoriety like her be interested in a simple guy from Queens? He turned the corner and walked toward the station floating on air. Never once had he felt like this. Was this falling in love—and falling hard? He hardly noticed the train and got on just in time, but all he wanted was her right now. If he had to quit his job, he was going to be here tomorrow. The doors closed to the train right behind him, and Tony found himself missing her already. Strangely he felt like there was something odd about Michelle he couldn't put his finger on. She was in his head, and all he wanted to do was find a way back her and soon. It was like she was intoxicating. He had no idea what was going on, but he had to be back here tomorrow night—not only to see her, but find out why he felt this way.

CHAPTER 5

Later that afternoon, Tony was talking to Kenny on the phone in his room in Queens, and he was hoping he wasn't going to be too upset he had gone to Manhattan without him, and to the Factory especially. Only a little while ago, he had called in sick and hoped it wasn't going to be a problem either, but in his mind, Tony was going to see Michelle again, and that was worth the risk. Still, he did need the job, and by calling in sick, someone was going to have to cover his shift tonight restocking the store.

"What do you mean you just called in sick! Dude, is this why I got called into work tonight?" Kenny yelled at Tony on the phone, now upset.

Just then Tony realized he shouldn't have called Kenny and that he was the one who had to cover his shift. Then he began to explain his night last night with Michelle and why he had to call in. Why he just had to go and see her again right away; it's all he had on his mind today. Even the pile of college applications his mother had left for him remained untouched.

"So, you're telling me that because of your love life, I get my day off taken away from me? This is some bullshit, Tony. And then I find out you're going to the city's most premier club again after you went there last night without your bro, your wingman. That's cold, man, that's just cold!" Kenny said back, and Tony could hear he sounded pretty upset too.

He felt horrible about this now; not only was he calling out sick, he just got his friend called in on his day off. "Look, I'll make it up to you, but I gotta do this. Ken, I'm falling for this girl, she's amazing, and oh my god, she's so beautiful and so smart..."

There was silence on the phone and then laughter—lots of it. "Dude, I'm fucking with you! I'm getting paid overtime tonight to go in, so go get her, man! Just make sure the next time you go there, you take me with you. I wanna be on one of those lists at least once in my miserable life," he said, still laughing loudly and realizing he had Tony stammering for the moment.

Hearing him, Tony almost hung up on him, and then he found the humor in it too. He promised to let him go next time and hoped he remembered to ask Michelle when he saw her tonight. Sometimes Kenny was a pain in the ass, but other times, he was a really good friend too. He took one step away from the phone in his room, and it rang again. Tony picked it up, and Chuck was asking him what he was up to tonight. But he didn't want to tell him about last night or tonight either. He was keeping his small relationship with Michelle quiet for now to avoid any problems. He told him, "Nothing much. I'm not feeling so good and need to sleep early." But Chuck then told him his ex was at home for the upcoming holidays. She wanted to see him, according to Liz, but Tony told him he hadn't heard from Ashley at all.

"Man, did you check your pager? She said she beeped you like five times," Chuck said, still thinking he was too hung up on something else to have missed that.

Tony looked around for his pager in his room and found it in his gym bag for martial arts. There were actually six pages and two messages and a voice mail. "Damn, man, I just noticed that my battery had died, and I left it in my bag. I'll call her tomorrow if I can, but I just feel like crap right now, seriously. I just called in sick too."

Chuck listened to him about a few things coming up and soon, how he had a tournament in a few days upstate, because he was trying to change the subject. He was traveling with some of the students in a day or so. In reality, he was looking for something decent in his closet to meet Michelle in.

"Okay, but she's looking for ya, and I think she's looking to get back together, dude. You can stop with the constant misery and with the black cloud you think you have over your head these days. Call her soon, and your blind date is quite upset she's back too. Brittney likes you since you stood up for her with that bitch at the club," he said, trying to cheer him up, and Tony just tossed a shirt to his bed. He knew it was better not to mention Michelle, and he was right. But now it seemed like he had three girls in the span of two days looking for him.

"Look, I'm gonna lay down, man. I'll call both of 'em soon enough, okay?" he said back, looking to get off the phone seeing what time it was.

"Okay, man, just don't forget, before you lose their interests. You know how chicks get, right?" Chuck said with another laugh.

"Yeah, I get ya, talk to ya later," Tony said quickly, and then he hung up; he knew all too well because he was going to see one soon too, and he was convinced he was going to look like a poor boy from Queens when he did.

*****

The sun had just barely set in SoHo, and Michelle was up already. She was ransacking her closet in her robe looking for something to wear that pleased her. Since meeting Tony, she had been using her abilities around him a lot. For the first time, this morning, she had let him leave without conditioning him to return. For that reason, she was a little nervous about being stood up tonight. He said he had to work, but she felt she was worth much more than a silly human job. Still, she had been tossing around clothes now for almost an hour and had yet to take a shower, let alone think about her makeup, hair, and jewelry tonight. She just couldn't get it out of her head that he might not show up. She had to keep reassuring herself in the mirrors of her closet who in their right mind would stand her up. She tried on yet another blouse and hated it. She then deposited it into the throwaway pile and continued to go through her closet still searching for something that could top the last few nights. Then it dawned on her while looking over a very scanty halter top that Tony wouldn't care about how perfect she was dressed; he would care more about her company. She had let him go without conditioning, so it's time to see what Tony really thought of her. She took out a very cute but very plain knee-high skirt, then she took out a beautiful but vintage white Chanel blouse. Finally, she found a pair of very nice but very conservative heels and didn't go with her signature stilettos. For her makeup, she went with softer tones, and her jewelry was very conservative too. Add in her very long leather jacket and her hair done up just right; she looked in the mirrors. Michelle liked what she saw; she had taken a little relaxation on her wardrobe, but it still said very classy, business chic meets social butterfly. She then grabbed her bag and headed for the front door. When she walked out, her driver had to look twice and make sure it was her. With a small laugh, she found this fun—going a little incognito from the party girl to more formal for once. If Tony truly liked her for her, this would tell her, so she began to think.

This time Michelle arrived at the club first, and she headed right for the second floor. She found the love seat they had used last night and sat back down. Next was the part she hated, waiting. It wasn't long until she spotted him, and when he saw her, she waved, and he had to look twice. Tony walked over and then smiled widely.

"Well, that's a very different look for you, Michelle," he said, sitting next to her.

This time he had brought her orchids, and she took them with a huge smile. But then she had to ask, "You didn't like me this time?"

He was the one who now laughed loudly and had to stop himself. "What, for your clothes? I could care, but I do appreciate it when you come dressed to impress. This is just new for me, but you look so distinguished. But yes, I do like it, because it's you, and it's hard for me to say this, but I missed you all day," he said as she took in the scent of the flowers he had brought her.

Michelle then took his hand and got closer to him. "You don't even know how good that makes me feel. I was hoping you'd be here too. I guess you got out of work for me?"

Tony told her the story of him calling in sick and then asked if she could put his friend Kenny on the lists once because he really wanted that. She agreed and then began to sit back and relax for a moment. She knew it: he wanted just her, and her money and prestige meant little. This made her quite happy, to say the least, for once in so long, a real friend.

"So which floor would you like to go to first?" she asked him, and then he thought for a moment.

"I'm thinking let's step out fast and hit a restaurant or something, I'm starved, and you look so damn good, I'd like to take you to a nice place," he said back, still enthralled by her.

Michelle then thought of the perfect place to go and got up. She took out her phone and dialed for her driver to come around to the front. As she walked out, she told him about this little bistro she knew of closer to Greenwich than Chelsea, so they would need a car. As they walked out, Michelle took his hand and walked closely to him due to the colder windy night. She was quite happy with this turn of events and felt that Tony belonged to her now. She wasn't letting anyone get in the way of that right now. In her eyes, what was hers stayed hers.

The bistro she was talking about was really in Greenwich and looked like it was full too. The car pulled up, and Michelle got out first and walked in without worry. She had asked Tony to stay in the car while she got them a table. When she walked out again, he expected bad news, but she told him to come with her instead. When they got inside, they were clearing a cozy table for two, with candles in a shaded far corner. Michelle sat first as Tony pulled out her chair. Again, she was impressed, because he never seemed to fail to surprise her with little things like that. Tony had manners too, rare for humans these days. After a round of both white and red wine, they moved on to appetizers, and as the bottle of white wine ran dry, she had a new one brought. They both ordered their entree and decided to go with something each of them could both share. Throughout appetizers, Michelle's phone constantly rang; and when they brought the second bottle of white, she just turned off her phone and tossed it into her purse. She didn't care about that or anything else right now other than who she was presently with.

They took their time eating dinner, and the chatting never ceased. Michelle was loving the idea of having dinner with a real friend. When the bill came, Tony reached for it, but Michelle put her hand over his and slipped the paper out from under his hand.

"My treat," she said as she took the check and held out her card to pay for dinner.

Once they had paid, Michelle caught Tony sneaking in the tip. She had the car brought back around by turning her phone back on. When the car arrived, Michelle got in first followed by Tony; and as the car left, she put her head on his shoulder and took his hand in hers. She had just closed her eyes, contented, when her stomach began to turn in a very bad way. Michelle thought she was going to be sick and let go of his hand suddenly. She had eaten at this restaurant before. *What can possibly be causing this?* she began to wonder. She then felt pain shoot through her lower chest, and she realized what this was. She hadn't fed in close to three nights, and she was getting ravenous! Tony was in more danger than he had ever been in his entire life right now. He was in the back of a car with an Immortal elder who was now using every ounce of willpower she had not to feed on him! Worse yet, if she didn't feed soon, this limousine could end up covered in blood with two bodies in it—the driver and Tony's too. As far as she was concerned, the car couldn't get back to the club fast enough!

When the car pulled up to the front doors, Michelle had to compose herself as she got out. She took his hand, and the two of them walked into the club quickly. She had to get away from him before the worst happened because she desperately needed to feed. The pain in her chest was only getting worse by the moment, and she needed to feed before she lost her composure completely. Michelle took Tony over to the first-floor bar and asked him to wait for her. Then she told him to put any drinks on her tab too. With that she walked past the black velvet ropes of the Abyss and down the stairs.

35

Tony watched her go and started to wonder about what people called the club inside a club. Most people here weren't allowed down there, but obviously she was. He turned and began to walk toward the bar to get a drink and wait for Michelle.

Meanwhile, Michelle hurried down the stairs quickly, and the white of the club above faded to the deep black below of the Abyss. When she got to the floor below, the low lights and black floors and walls greeted her. She made her way right toward the main pillar that obscured the room beyond. There carved into the black pillar was the image of Baphomet, the horned god; and above that, the image of Lilith, the demon queen of both the Succubus and Incubus caste. Michelle walked right past and practically ran into Elijah, of all people, as she entered the main room. He didn't look happy at all and scowled when he saw her.

"There you are, and where in God's name have you been? I've been calling you for hours, and then your phone gets turned off. Michelle, I need these problems like a hole in my fucking chest! You better have a really good excuse because I'm listening," he said annoyed. But Michelle said nothing back and tried to walk past him, but he put out his arm inhumanly fast. "Now, Michelle, and I'm listening," Elijah said adamantly and narrowed his gaze at her.

She glanced up at him with a nervous look in her eyes. "I can't right now, Elijah…and you shouldn't be around me either," she snapped back, closing her eyes and grimacing in pain.

Elijah saw his prodigy in agony and walked her to the far corner near the pillar. "What's going on, tell me right now," he asked when they were far away from others.

"Elijah, I'm in trouble… I'm borderline ravenous! I haven't fed for three nights… I need to hunt now because… I'm close killing someone," she said back, grabbing her side again and almost toppled over.

Elijah grabbed her, and he could hear the low growls beginning. Her willpower was failing her, and how she hadn't attacked him was amazing. He put his arm around her unafraid and walked to the hidden door in the Abyss that allowed Immortals to move between floors unnoticed. He opened the heavy door and walked with her up the hidden industrial iron staircase to the third floor, where the most people were usually congregated by now. He had to watch over her now because if he didn't, someone was going to die horribly tonight; and in the club, that was never a good thing when it came to business.

A short while later, on the third floor, Michelle exploded out of the shadows and grabbed a lone man from behind, and his drink tumbled to the floor. She tossed him against the dark wall, stunning him. Her forked and bladed tongue shot out her mouth, and she drilled her vicious thorn into his chest, piercing his aorta with the ease of a surgeon's scalpel. The barbed shorter fangs of her split tongue clamped down hard and embedded into his flesh. Then a long tongue and thorn burrowed in deeper under his skin. She tapped into his essence in his blood and began to feed viciously. It wasn't the blood she wanted, it was the essence or life force she desired, and it called to her. Her tongue siphoned the life force with ease and drew it out into her body. The man tried to struggle, but he simply wasn't strong enough, and her smaller fangs at the tips of her tongue were coated in a fast-acting aesthetic. Michelle's heart suddenly reversed, and she began to feed, rapidly drawing out his essence with it. Elijah watched on but rushed over to her telling her she was going to kill him, but she hardly heard him. She continued to feed, and suddenly Elijah pulled Michelle off him before she consumed his entire soul! He shook her by the shoulders to snap her out of it, and she came out of her frenzy.

"Damn it, Michelle, get a grip! You nearly not only killed him but tore out his soul! Not in a fucking club, and you know better too, damn it," he said, and Michelle shook her head, and Elijah let go of her then.

She closed the wound with a bit of her hot black blood from her own lip and her split tongue holding the incision closed. She then looked out toward the crowd again. She wasn't done, not by a long shot, she thought. As her long tongue licked away the remnants of her last meal from her lips and chin, the blood was sweet, but it did little to appease her. It was the essence that called to her, and her demon demanded more too.

About an hour later, Michelle drew in a deep breath and then looked down at her third victim of the night and exhaled slowly. She had already closed his wound, and she had fed softly on him because she had only pierced his jugular vein. She licked the last amount of blood off her lip, and it was so full of essence it eased her heart rate further. The danger had passed, and she was sated again. She then scanned the crowd, and no one had seen a thing in the darkness of the rave. The glow of neon lights and the rhythmic pulse of the music brought her back to a lucid state. She then noticed Elijah motioning to her near the hidden door, and she walked that way because she owed him an explanation. Begrudgingly she made her way to the door because she knew what was coming next. Once inside, Elijah closed the heavy door with a thud and locked it again, and then he turned toward her still angry.

"Now, you're going to tell me why you not only ignored your damn phone and then turned it off. But more importantly the reason for you not feeding for three damn nights. Damn it, Michelle, I had to haul you off someone, or you would have finished him. You know better, I don't need ravenous Immortals in the damn club, it causes small problems, like fucking bodies! So, start explaining right now," he said quickly and was still upset about before.

She didn't want to and decided to leave and tried to walk past him, but he grabbed her shoulder, stopping her. Normally Michelle would get quite mad for something like that. But this was her creator, and as suave and debonair as Elijah could be, a true ladies' man, he could also be a cold and savage fighter and not someone you angered if you could help it. Last time she watched him deal with someone this angry, there were no words spoken. Elijah simply tore off the man's head and then ripped him in half with his bare hands! That moment still stuck with her to this day because the look on his face afterward made her realize that it wasn't something he hadn't seen or done before; truly frightening, to say the least—his expression, not the act.

"I said *now*, and I meant it, and so help me if you shadow-walk, I will find you tonight, and you will be very sorry. My generous mood from before is waning quickly, Michelle, and any more might

IN THE NAME OF SIN

make tonight unpleasant for you, to put it lightly," he said back to her, now looking her right in the eyes as his narrowed.

Michelle frowned back but started to tell Elijah about her nights with her new friend Tony and how it had distracted her. He shook his head hearing the story, and together they began to walk down the iron stairs in the darkness of the passageway. Once they arrived at the door for floor 1, he stopped before he unlocked the secret door.

"I care little how you spend your time, Michelle, but when you do things like this that could jeopardize this club and every Immortal in the city, I care a lot. Now come and introduce me to your new friend, and also what's your plans with him. Your human pets' usual don't last long most days," he said sternly, and she never liked how he referred to the humans she took a fancy to.

Michelle walked toward the door as he opened it, and she looked back. "He's not a pet, you know, he's…my friend. Remember this, Elijah," she said back, annoyed, but Elijah knew that Immortals couldn't afford them most times though, especially human ones.

Above on the first floor, it had been over an hour since Tony had seen Michelle. He was beginning to wonder if she was coming back at all. He was considering leaving because he wasn't interested in another drink right now. He stood up and tossed a tip on the bar for the few beers he drank, but from behind, Michelle wrapped her arms around him, surprising him.

"You weren't thinking of leaving me, were you?" she asked as she let him go.

He turned to face her, and she looked a lot better than before when they got back to the club. Tony was starting to wonder about who was calling her phone like that or if she was sick from the food they just ate.

"I'm so sorry, but I had pressing matters that needed taking care of immediately when we got back. Thank you for waiting for me," she explained quickly and then kissed his cheek.

Together they began to walk to the far end of the bar. Michelle really didn't want to do this, but she didn't have a choice either; Elijah had just helped her. When they arrived, she tapped Elijah on the shoulder, and he stood up slowly and turned.

"Tony, I'd like you to meet my older brother Elijah Quintus Du'Pree. He's the owner of the Factory and kind of my boss. He was the one who was calling before and demanded to meet the man that had lured his sister out of the club on a busy night. He was the one calling my phone at the bistro, and that's why I had to rush off when we got back," she said, and now Tony thought this was trouble if he had gotten Michelle into some here.

Elijah was an imposing figure, very tall and quite well-built; his auburn, red hair and goatee were both well-kept. But it was his strange light-grayish-green eyes that seemed to have a glow to him that was his defining feature. He shared some of the same facial features with Michelle too, as if handsome hardly befit him in the least. Then he grinned a bit, which seemed to immediately put at ease what seemed to be a tense situation just then. Elijah put out his strong hand, and Tony took it without fear, hoping he hadn't caused a problem tonight.

"Oh, I like this one, Michelle, he has a firm handshake and no fear in his eyes. Consider yourself my guest, and I'll put you on my list so you can come and go from the club and see my sister when you like as well. This way you don't have to stand in those ridiculous lines, like tonight," he said back, holding a single finger up to the bartender; and in a moment, he set a glass down.

Tony thanked him and asked him to sit with them, but he refused but appreciated the offer. He then picked up his drink from the bar, a whiskey sour, neat, and walked past Michelle and Tony, heading out of the first floor.

"Enjoy your night, you two, but keep your phone on this time. By the way, Tony, be careful with her, you've seen her sweet side, but you don't want to see the sour one. I'll take my leave, good evening," he said and walked off toward the ropes to the Abyss again.

Michelle, on the other hand, knew what he was up to. Elijah put Tony's name on his list, which was good because he was protected here now from other Immortals. But he was now able to keep tabs on him too. If he couldn't keep tabs on Michelle, he would keep tabs on her new friend. Regardless, she wasn't going to let this ruin her night. She led him to her favorite table on this floor, and they sat again, resuming their night.

CHAPTER 6

A few hours later, Michelle and Tony we're outside the club sharing a long and very passionate kiss. She didn't want this to end, and she ran her fingers through his hair gently. This time she was the one floating on air tonight. It had been so long since she felt like this. They finished their kiss, and once again she invited him to be her guest at her home, but again he said no. She wanted him badly right now; she had just fed too, and it would just be sweet lovemaking, which a Succubus was exquisite at. Still, he respected her too much, and his own honor wouldn't allow him to cheapen her like that; to Tony, she was a lady—he'd never even consider defiling that. Once again, not only had he refused her but amazed her with his sense of virtue that he held so dear. She let him go and accepted the fact that she would slumber alone yet again. Part of her was upset, but part of her liked the idea that Tony had that much respect for her in his heart. She asked him if she would see him tonight, but he had said no again. He had to go out of town and would be back tomorrow, and he'd come by then. Michelle gave him her private numbers and got his beeper number from him with a little coaxing. She hated to see him go, and once again her thoughts went back to where this would go or, worse yet, end. She couldn't stop thinking, Had she found him, finally, after all these long years, the one? But she laughed it off as he walked away; she was cursed, and her curse was loneliness, one she accepted a long time ago. Michelle then watched him turn the corner and walked back into the club to deal with Elijah, again.

Around the corner, Tony felt like a total idiot yet again. She had invited him to her place twice, and he turned her down. He had to be out of his mind, but he felt such an attraction to her, but he didn't want to cheapen it with one night of meaningless sex. He truly liked Michelle and then realized he had fallen in love with her deeply. He had nothing to offer her though. He was a poor boy from Queens that had very little in life. Tony wasn't stupid; he had seen how Elijah had looked at him, as a pauper that had no business with an upscale socialite like his sister, Michelle Du'Pree. He was even convinced now that sooner or later Michelle would realize she was slumming and disappear too. Still, he hoped that his luck had finally changed somehow. Sometimes he felt like he was cursed with bad luck because nothing ever stayed put in his life. He turned down the stairs into the subway station that would take him home and walked past the turnstiles. He couldn't stop thinking, *Don't fall this hard for her, it's not going to end well, and you've got to be able to recover from it afterward.* Life didn't end after yet another bout of bad luck. The train pulled in, and Tony walked in at the edge of both joy and sadness; he knew where this was going to end, and he was just trying to prepare himself for what he thought was inevitable. The doors slid closed, and the train began to take him back to reality.

It had been two days now since Michelle had heard anything from Tony, and he had said one, and she wasn't happy. The first night at the club hadn't been very fun for her at all because it was surrounded by sadness and longing. Honestly, as Elijah put it, she was moping around the club all night. Not only was she upset, but she didn't even want to raise any hell either, something she was legendary at the club for. But Elijah had grown quite accustomed to her when it came to a moody Michelle, but this was a bit much even for him. For most of that night, she was just sitting around in the Abyss not really doing much; but when she did, it was only because someone or something angered her. In all, she looked quite lost and despondent though. She continually checked both her watch and her phone periodically but said very little beyond screaming at someone. Now it was the second night, and not one word from Tony. If he was with that little brunette skank from the first night at the club, Michelle would kill her just for messing with what was rightfully hers in her opinion. Instead of going to the club and waste yet another night just brooding, she had every intention of going looking for him. Michelle had to see for herself he wasn't standing her up or ignoring her. She had tried his pager a few times last night, but nothing had been returned. Now she was going to go looking for him. She knew he lived in Queens, but that was a big place; she needed a bit more information first. And then she got a very devious idea. She called over to the club and checked if his friend had used his spot on her list yet. She found out he had used it, tonight. If there was any way to get information, he would be the perfect place to start. She decided to get dressed and head over. She also called the garage and asked that her red classic Ferrari Testarossa be brought by because she was driving herself tonight too; she was in the mood.

Later on, when Michelle arrived at the club, she walked right past security with a very angry stride. Most of the employees could see she was not in a good mood, and her reputation preceded her. As she walked along the white marble floors of the first level, a couple got in front of her, but she shoved both of them out of her way without stopping. She headed right to one of the most helpful places in the club, personal belongings or the coat check room. Michelle walked right up to the counter and drummed her fingertips on it, but no one moved until she slammed her fist into it, getting their full attention. Most of them knew just who she was and decided it was time to get back to work. She then asked one of the people if a certain someone checked personal property. They looked down the lists, and she pointed out his name and grinned. She then told them to bring her the jacket because it was just what she needed. Michelle waited a moment and snatched the jacket and began to go through the pockets. She found little, but that didn't matter. She handed the jacket back and then told them all she was never here. Once she was far enough away from the counter, she sniffed her hands while faking to fix her hair. She had his scent now, Tony's friend Kenny, that was, and she ducked into a shadow and vanished swiftly.

Up on the fourth floor, Kenny was having a blast at the concert tonight. Tony had come through with his name on a list, and he got in even without a cover charge or a ticket for the show. He was now hanging out with a few girls and thought this place was the greatest. What he didn't see was Michelle locked on to his aura after she had gotten his scent, and she made a straight line right toward him. He was going to tell her where Tony was, or she was going to hurt him bad before she killed him. Tony was hers, and if anything got in her way, she wasn't in the mood tonight. She walked right past the girls he was with and, with one cold look, scared most of them off, but then one decided to test her. Michelle slapped her so hard she nearly bounced off the floor. Then she turned her attention toward Kenny.

"Do you know who I am?" she asked him furiously and stared right through him.

Kenny backed up a little bit and realized who she was, and Tony was in big trouble too. "You're that girl from the club he's been seeing lately...Michelle...right?"

Without a word, she grabbed him by the collar and walked him over to a quieter place. Once there, she got right down to business. Michelle was going to get information out of him; she could see his aura, and he was quite afraid of her too. Good, she thought, he was smart.

"I haven't seen or heard from Tony in two days now. I want to know where he is, who he's with, or where I can find him, RIGHT NOW!" she said so hostilely it even made Kenny worried.

She was so hot but so damn mean. What had his friend got himself into, Kenny thought to herself. "Well, I've got no idea where he is right now or why he'd ditch you either. But I hope you find him, good luck," he replied and then began to walk back to the concert.

Quickly Michelle put out her arm, blocking his way. "Not so fast. And, Kenny, if he's cheating on me, I promise you I'll deal with him when I find him, but right now, we're not done," she said, stopping him in his tracks again.

In a little while, she had Tony's home address and his martial arts studio's address too, which she snatched the card from him. Kenny said it was his only one, but Michelle hardly cared. Finally,

IN THE NAME OF SIN

they both worked at the same place, and she found out where that was too. In the end, Michelle let him go, but not without warning him that if he had lied, she was coming back. Kenny swore up and down he hadn't, and then Michelle suggested, "You might want to find your friend, and soon too." Because if he was two-timing her, Tony was about to be the sorriest he had ever been in his entire life. She then let him go, and Kenny was worried for his friend because he was involved with a royally pissed-off rich bitch on a rampage that sounded like she would kill him.

After finishing getting the information she needed, Michelle was leaving, but she decided first to stop in the Abyss and tell Elijah she was stepping out for the night. She had some personal things to deal with, and she needed to see them through. Luckily, even with the live music, it wasn't a busy night. When she got down the stairs and around the column, she saw Elijah at the bar and headed toward him. But she ran into one Immortal in particular she absolutely disliked. Iris Sulteran was an elder of a different demonic caste called Bael or Envy Demons, but of a lower house in the city, still an elder in her own right and powerful enough. She had a gripe with Michelle that was over seventy years old, and for the life of her, she didn't know what it was about anymore. She walked past her, and then Iris decided to say something to her at the wrong time.

"I saw you down here last night, Mish, and you looked absolutely miserable too. What happened, your newest boy toy got away from you? Hmmm? Are you losing your touch, Mish, or is it that you just forgot how to seduce anymore? Funny, a little Succubus that can't use lust correctly, are you going to starve?" she asked her condescendingly, and Michelle seethed with rage; she hated her right now.

Michelle whirled around and stared her down, and everyone knew how much she hated her name shortened like that. Insulting her in the city of New York was never a good idea, but Iris was pushing her luck in the Abyss—even with Elijah around—thinking she was safe. Tonight though, she thought wrong; Michelle was in a foul mood, and most people steered clear of her then.

"You started that rumor, Iris, and we all know it's you who has problems getting a regular meal here at the club. You might want to head up and get to work drawing in the envy because when it comes to you, it takes that much time. Look at how you dressed. Hurry up before you go hungry yet again. No sense about fashion or anything else either. Do yourself a favor, fire your stylist," Michelle snapped back, walking closer to Elijah, but then she heard a voice she didn't want to hear again.

"Aww, Mish, I even heard your creator had to put protection on him so you could get a chance to feed. Too bad he's not upstairs tonight. Take off the protection, and I'll show you how it's done. Maybe lust doesn't do it for him. Let me try. Besides, you're the one looking a little envious tonight, hmmm?" she said back, laughing at her still.

Elijah then saw that ever-familiar gleam in his prodigy's eyes that usually resulted in very expensive damages to the club and shook his head with a sigh. Michelle turned again and stared her down with a loud growl escaping her lips.

"Say that to my face, you low-born-blood Bael BITCH," she snarled in a full rage.

"You're a has-been, Mish, or a never was. You know it, and so do I, you lustful little WHORE," she said back, laughing, then growled menacingly.

Michelle took one more deep breath; there was that word she loathed the most, *whore*. And without warning, she screamed the word *bitch* right at Iris. She sent her tumbling backward and clearing tables and chairs away on the floor from the force of the hellish scream. But Iris got up fast, and both of them took off at inhuman speed and met in the center of the room as members filed out of the Abyss quickly. Two enraged demonesses were about to go to blows! Iris punched Michelle hard, and she had forgotten how strong she was. And Michelle tumbled to the floor but fell through the shadows and came at Iris from the left with her wicked claws bared. Iris screamed as she felt them rake down her back, leaving behind bloody gouges and gashes. Iris howled in pain when she felt the poison from them too. Michelle pressed her advantage, slicing the back of her leg viciously and left a wide deep slash. Thick black oily blood sprayed from the wound and steamed on the floors, turning quickly to ash.

Michelle moved away fast, avoiding the horrible spray of smoking oily blood. Iris whirled around and swung hard at her, hitting her solidly in the chest, and then melted away, becoming a wisp of steam. Michelle in response dove into the next shadow and vanished as well. Iris became solid again, and when Michelle reemerged from the shadows, she used illusions to turn the room upside down and then used a projection of her will to batter her mind. While she was stunned, Michelle dove through another shadow and grabbed Iris, hauling her with her through another shadow. Together they tumbled out of a shadow from the ceiling, and Iris was in agony, but she grabbed Michelle and tossed her to the floor, hard enough to crack the marble, and then the very ground began to ripple from the hit, looking like it was melting, and Iris was trying to force her into the liquid stone she had created.

"Bye-bye, Mish," she hissed back, pressing her into the stone that looked like melted marble.

Elijah ran in to break it up because he saw Iris was about to feed on Michelle once she trapped her! Bael was the only caste that could draw sustenance from another Immortal! But Michelle grinned back and then melted through the floor's shadows. She reappeared from the ceiling once again and landed on Iris, punching her in the back of the head hard. She fell to the ground with a splatter, and Michelle stepped over her and reached down and grabbed her long tongue still out with her taloned hand. Elijah was disoriented from the illusion fading suddenly and could only watch on in horror of what was going to happen next! He yelled out for her to stop, but Michelle was hardly listening; she was so angry.

"Enjoy synthetic, you fucking little Bael bitch!" she screamed and tore out her tongue, thorn included, with a loud wet tearing sound.

Black steaming bitter blood sprayed out of Iris's mouth, and Michelle tossed the tongue to the ground and watched as it sizzled and melted away. She kicked Iris over and raised her clawed hand to finish her as Iris raised her arms and turned her head waiting for the killing blow. But before the strike came, Elijah grabbed Michelle and threw her to the side before she could. Michelle got up and saw her creator attending to her enemy and headed right for the doorway.

"Michelle, get back here right now this instant!" he screamed at her seeing the mess Iris was.

But Michelle never looked back and flipped off her creator and Iris as she walked into another looming shadow. She wasn't going to help that bitch, not after calling her a whore. As far as she was concerned, next time she saw Iris, she was dead!

Outside the club, Michelle got into her Ferrari and hit the gas hard, leaving rubber on the road outside the Factory. She was furious and in a total rage right now because she was convinced Tony was cheating on her. Her creator had just taken that bitch Iris's side after that fight too. She tore through the city heading right for Queens, and she was heading right for Tony's home absolutely furious. It took a little bit of time, but she finally arrived in Tony's neighborhood and parked her car a little way away from his house. She stomped her way right back to his house and had a good mind to kick in his front door too; she was in such a rage. As she walked up to the door, there was a pungent odor in the air, and she stopped short in her tracks. Michelle then glanced around, and then she saw it in the front yard, sage plants! Sage was very dangerous to Immortals, and thankfully she had smelled it because it knocked her back to her senses. She didn't know for sure if he was two-timing her, and smashing his door open wasn't the best way to confront him. There would also be a lot of explaining to do afterward, about how she smashed open a heavy front door. Michelle then realized she needed to find him and speak to him first before she accused him of anything. She then decided to head around back and see if there was another way in and around the sage instead.

CHAPTER

7

When Michelle headed around back, she was lucky there were no sage plants growing back here. Sage had so many uses against Immortals: the oil caused caustic burns, the odor kept them away because it was offensive, and the smoke was like a chemical Mace that would repel them for up to three days but also made them violently sick. The worst was if it got into their blood, it caused absolute havoc with their anatomy, and the pain was unbearable. Avoiding it was always the best option, at all costs too. She peered into a window, and there she saw a big-enough shadow on the living room wall. Michelle then headed farther into backyard and found a suitable shadow there on the back wall. She glanced around again, then she walked through the shadow slowly and stepped silently into the living room cautiously. Instantly she then knelt down quickly and put her hand on the floor subtly. Suddenly she knew the entire floor plan of the house and exactly where Tony's small room was too. She had drawn this information out of the energy trapped in the house itself.

Immortals could tap into residual energy as easily as they did life energy. Michelle learned long ago everything held energy; it surrounded all living things, and it could all be very useful. She could even see it when she wished. But she also found out she wasn't alone here this way too. From the room opposite his, there was someone asleep inside; she sensed life energy or essence. Now Michelle moved cautiously toward the hall and looked right into the nearest room, and someone moved in the bed. She sniffed the air and guessed Tony must have had a younger sister. Michelle gently pulled the door close, hoping it didn't squeak while she did. She was prepared to wipe this girl's mind if need be, but better to not take chances. She made her way to the next room and glided inside, softly shutting the door silently behind her. There was a scent in the air of a girl she didn't recognize, and she frowned at first. But then snatching the photo on his desk in a small portrait frame, she realized this must be the ex he told her about. Of course, her residual scent would be in here, she thought. He had told her how long they were a couple. Michelle then began to snoop around and found a few pieces of paper with a few numbers she might be able to use, his friends'. She slid those into her pocket and next went through his very small closet, which was heavy with her perfume, roses, and jasmine oils, making her realize the other scent was much older, and she realized she had been the one he was with most recently with, and now she grinned. As she continued to search, she heard the front door open and saw the living room light turned on. She wasn't ready to have Tony find her waiting in his room just yet. She took one more look at the portrait and flipped it facedown.

"He traded up, bitch," Michelle whispered and stepped through a shadow in his room.

In a moment, she reappeared out in the yard where she had initially entered from. Michelle then looked back in the window and realized it wasn't Tony; it had to be his mother. She decided it was time to cut her losses and head back to her car before she was seen.

When Michelle got to her car, she took off before something else happened here or she was noticed. She didn't need something that could alert Tony to her presence here tonight. Hopefully no one who knew Tony or his family had seen her car here, because a red Ferrari Testarossa was out of place here. From here she took the business card she had confiscated from Kenny and drove to his martial arts academy, which wasn't far from his house. When she got there, she noticed a huge problem right away; the entire front of the building was all glass. She guessed it was like that to draw in potential business so people passing by could watch a class being instructed. She walked over to the glass and saw the entire wall to the right was a giant shadow. She had an entry point, but anyone walking by would see her do so. She walked around back, and there were no windows to look into though. She then touched the side of the building, and like at his house, she had the floor plans and such but not where the shadows were, and there was no one inside right now either. She knew where to go, and Tony had a locker in the back room; she sensed his residual energy there. She decided to risk being seen and stepped through a shadow in the back of the building and into the studio. With all the speed she had, she rushed like a blur into the back locker room.

Next Michelle headed right for his locker but found it locked. It meant little to her, and she tugged the door once, and it opened up easily. She then used her fingers to bend the metal back into place so when she closed the door again, it would lock well enough. Then she began to go through his locker and found a flier for a tournament upstate, but that was yesterday. She also realized this tournament was for kids eight to sixteen years old. So Tony must have had his black belt in order to teach, she thought. She went through his stuff in a bag in the locker and found what she thought she would, a black belt with a thin gold stripe. He had never told her any of this and that he taught, and children too. She continued to go through his bag and found a beat-up day planner. Slowly she began flipping through the months and saw he had two days blocked off this month, yesterday and today. She then began to wonder why two days for a one-day tournament. While she went through the rest of his locker, she had found a paper bracelet from the club used to identify who could drink from the bars. Her scent was heavy on it, and he cared enough to keep this even though most people threw them away. Michelle then found another picture of a few people, and Tony was in it with his ex on his shoulders. Once again, her blood boiled, and she tore the picture in half and stuffed it in her pocket. If he was with her tonight, she was going to kill them both. She closed the locker again and checked that it locked; it did. Michelle then walked into a shadow and out into the back of the building. She had one more place to check: his job. She walked back to her car and was headed there next. Still, why two days for a one-day tournament, she began to wonder. Tony had told her about his ex and how she had broken up with him days before she left for school. Was she going to a college in the area near the tournament grounds, and were they planning to meet to try to reconcile? Michelle then scowled at that thought; if that was the case, it was going to be the shortest reconciliation in the history of the world because when she was done, they would both need a funeral next.

CHAPTER 8

An hour later, Michelle realized why she hated the mall and despised Queens that much more now. Never once had she ever been so disgusted by the looks of the people around her. How humans lived like this was a mystery to her. The sights and smells of this place made her enhanced senses want to gag. She was also dressed wrong too; her expensive Prada clothes, handmade Italian leather boots, along with her custom Louis Vuitton jacket, Gucci handbag, and even her hair was a dead giveaway for a little rich girl. It took her a bit to find the department store that Tony worked at, but when she did, once again, she wasn't happy.

As she walked into the big box department store with its bright lights and long shelves that led down even longer aisles, she shook her head. She reviled the place, and Michelle couldn't understand how humans did it, slaved away their short lives like this.

"How do they live this way?" she muttered and continued on her way. "Someone has to work in this pigsty," she grumbled once more, and the bright lights hurt her very sensitive eyes.

Michelle then passed by a small mirror and glanced into it and realized she was so out of place right now. For once, she didn't belong somewhere, and it made her so uncomfortable. What was more concerning was that under these bright lights, the shadows were so small. Not much of an opportunity to escape if she wanted to leave fast.

Worse yet, none of these shadows would allow her to use any of her illusions if she wanted too either. Luckily, she hadn't used one when she entered because under these bright lights, holding it in place would've been near impossible. She yearned for the cool dark night and the fresh air again—well, as fresh as Queens allowed, she thought to herself. After a few more moments, she found what she was looking for: a few employees slaving away and wasting their short lives. She made her way toward them and cleared her throat to get their attention. Both of them looked right back at her, and Michelle let lust flow from her, and it snared both of their minds with ease as it overtook them.

"I'm hoping one of you could help me tonight. I'm looking for an employee here, his name is Tony Willhiem. Could you let me know if he's working tonight? If so, could I have a word with him?" she said as sweetly as she could right now.

Michelle was trying to sway them with her soft voice, but both of them seemed more confused right now than anything else. She tapped her boot on the scuffed floors to get them to stop staring. Then she realized her presence was too much and clouding their minds utterly, and she backed it off. That seemed to shake the taller one out of his lust-filled stupor; this was the power of her demonic caste, the Succubus and Incubus—presence and lust and being able to manipulate it. It was a useful tool, and when done right, it could cloud minds and lull the lustful with ease.

"Tony? Umm, I don't know a Tony here, but we have an Antonio that works here in the back, is that who you're looking for?" the one employee said that seemed to shake off his stupor first.

Michelle smiled back and then guessed it was. "I would think so. Is he here?" she asked him as cordially as she could, still playing on the pleasure centers of his feeble mind.

"Umm, no, he isn't working tonight, and he took two days off for a tournament upstate in case the kids made the finals. I guess they did since he's not here tonight. I bet we could help you out if you need something," he said back, winking at her playfully.

Michelle just frowned and realized this was the best he could do to flirt with her, how pitiful. She shook her head and backed away her lust some more, allowing the two of them to think a bit more clearly.

"No, I was looking for him to ask him something more specific. I don't need anything here, but thank you," she said back with a small sneer and began to turn to walk away.

Then she realized a small mistake she just made and turned back around again. Both of them were still enamored with her, and Michelle concentrated then used her will forcefully and made sure to speak loud enough for them to hear her with ease. She was using another of her mental talents; she could exert her will over someone from a distance if she could see their eyes. Some people liked to call it a *push* or a mental push. Either way, it was hard to resist when the mind was clouded already.

"Now, boys, you will forget you saw me, and Antonio will not find out I was here, correct?" she said, waving her finger and licking her lips slightly, sending a force of will that sent a wave of suggestion into their lust-clouded minds.

Both of their eyes glazed over for a moment, and Michelle quickly reversed her presence through her talents with lust and walked away from the aisle and headed for the doorway. She had sent a mental command to each of them, and the confusion of her presence was enough to make the suggestion very hard to ignore. The light from above in the store still hurt her sensitive eyes, and she was happy to get back to the darker hallways of the mall again for once in her life.

Once she had gotten her answers, she was sure he wasn't two-timing her, but she felt horrible now too for doubting Tony. He was helping some young kids at a tournament, and once again, he amazed her with his generosity and lack of selfishness. Michelle felt the need to leave here, and soon she felt she violated his trust entirely. It also felt like eyes were on her constantly, like everyone was scrutinizing her for just that. Again, she felt out of place and walked past the food court on her way out. But she stopped for a moment to get a good look at what Tony called food, his job, and his life. The sight upset her greatly. Tony was kind to her and wanted nothing from her other than companionship. It made him rare indeed; most people looking at her in this place saw things much differently. She was breathtakingly beautiful—that was evident, but it was obvious she had money and respect too, and that's what these people coveted more than her companionship. They wanted not only her affections but what she could give them if they swayed her. Tony hadn't tried to do that; he didn't belong with them, humans, that is. A person of his caliber and poise was too good for this entire place. She started to walk again, this time in the direction she had taken to get into this dump in the first place. She then made a quick decision; depending on how things went soon, Tony wasn't going back to the world of humans. They didn't deserve his mere presence. She was going to turn him or, if she had to, kill him. Better for him to be dead than deal with these parasites that would slowly destroy what integrity he had in his heart. Just then Michelle began to think once more. Had she found him, that one? But once more she shook her head. That never went well…ever.

Once outside, Michelle felt only slightly better. Inside the mall had been a disgusting eye-opener that made her realize how much she really hated human beings these days. She thought back to her day that she accepted what she was and left that world behind. Yes, she had given up the light; she had blackened her soul with what she was now, but the fall from her grace, to her, was well worth it. As Anneke had called it when she met her for the first time changed, a demoness or a female demon, also known as a Succubus, for her particular caste. At first the words had frightened her, but then she had come to realize it was better to be that than a human being. The power that came with it was so worth it. Michelle had changed her entire life and aspects through it. Humans treated each other with such malice and contempt for little reason. Yes, her dark world could be just as cruel if not more, but you had to bring that upon yourself most times; other times, it was humans who brought their cruelty to her world. She was now headed for the parking garage, and she wanted to get to her car and get out of here as quickly as she could; this place got more disgusting by the moment in her eyes.

Inside the underground parking garage, Michelle knew she wasn't alone; luckily the darkness was more home to her than anyone else in here. She took a deep breath and realized whatever it was following her was close by. She continued on unfazed and then slid her hand down one of the columns and closed her eyes for a moment as she passed by. Within that split second, she knew the layout, where she was, and how to get to anywhere she wanted to. Her keen hearing then picked up on footsteps from behind; her guess was between five and six different ones due to the echoes of the garage. Within moments, Michelle knew more about what was stalking her than they did about her. With a grin upon her lips, she decided to head down into the underground level even though her car was on the ground level. But darkness was her friend, and with that and no prying eyes, she could maybe make something out of this small inconvenience. At best it could be a meal for her, and her grin spread to a wide smile; she had never gotten takeout at a mall before.

Once Michelle had headed down to the next level, her senses told her that the group following her had split up now. Part of them had gone in a direction that would get in front of her within a few moments. She also knew that a few were still following her from behind, pushing her toward the other group that had split off. In response, Michelle moved to the left, past a few parked cars. The ones behind her followed, and this was almost too easy for her in a comical way. She could easily vanish in a shadow and get behind her pursuers, but she was slowly leading them toward the center of the garage; she wanted them all together for an easier target. Michelle felt it was best to face them all there, since there would be no one around and the shadows would be heavy there too. They thought they were the predators, but Michelle was leading her quarry like an alpha predator. Both Anneke and Elijah had taught her well how to set a trap and spring it. When she had finally come to the center of the garage and turned toward the ramp going up, she saw the first of them; three men blocked her path, so in a ruse, she doubled back, making it look like she was fleeing. They stupidly followed her, and Michelle listened for the footfalls from the ones who had been following her at first, who were now in front of her. They were so close but didn't realize the trap she was setting. All Michelle wanted was for them all to be in the center of the garage, where she could deal with them in the blackness. Just then she smelled a scent that she knew well, gun oil; at least one of them had a gun. This just kept getting better in her eyes; humans felt superior when they had firearms. It usually led to big mistakes that she planned to exploit too.

A few minutes later, in front of her, she heard a laugh and saw shadows blocking her path to the stairs, and they had her cornered, or so they thought, but Michelle's trap was about to slam shut. Then out of the corner of her eye, she saw the others, four of them, that had been following her, so there were seven. They must have felt so superior right now with their numbers and weapons. Then she heard the first of them call out to her from the musty old concrete garage, and his voice echoed off the solid walls.

"It's over, bitch, so come out. You can't go up from the ramp or the stairs," he said with a chuckle, trying to scare her.

Michelle then stopped walking and let her pursuers close in, and she was in the center of the lower level of the garage, right where she wanted to be. She tapped her foot and watched as they began to surround her and thought to herself, *That's it, you fool, get closer. I smell the gun, and I see the knives, and I sense my surroundings, but you've got no idea what's coming next, do you?* She was trying not to laugh and ruin the trap, and Michelle watched as they closed the distance slowly.

The next one spoke with the click of a switchblade. "Okay, bitch, you know where this is going next: money and maybe a little fun too. What do ya think?" he said, forcefully brandishing the knife in front of him.

Michelle tried to look frightened and held her arms to the side of her with hands open. "So, you want money, and you plan to rape me—just so I've got this straight. Is that it, boys?" she said, setting her purse on the ground carefully.

One of them answered her back smugly then, "Bingo, give the well-dressed whore a prize!"

Then another laughed. "We saw you strutting around the mall. Bet you don't feel so cocky now, do you, bitch?"

Michelle took a step forward and then closed her eyes and thought, *Wrong word to use tonight.* "Okay, let's get this over with then," she said with a sigh, and that's when one of them grabbed her from behind, trying to restrain her, and it was hard not to giggle.

Michelle felt her arms being attempted to be pinned behind her as the rest of them came rushing in, and she faked struggling to lure all of them in, and it was working. They were all too close now and well within striking distance. With ease, Michelle broke her attacker's grip and shoved him away hard. But another rushed her, and Michelle just stepped to the side and stuck out her arm. The force of the collision sent him spiraling to the ground with a loud crack. Another one with a knife attacked her, but Michelle moved so fast, dodging the blade, and then grabbed his arm; and with a wicked smile on her lips, she tossed him up into the air hard, and he slammed into the ceiling, only to fall face-first to the dirty concrete below. Then she felt something slip into her side, and it hurt for a moment. Someone had stabbed her, and now playtime was over!

"That's a one-of-a-kind Louis Vuitton jacket, you fucking asshole, and now it's got a fucking hole and blood on it!" she screamed out in fury now that her new jacket was damaged.

"Least of your worries right now, bitch," someone yelled back at her.

Just then someone rushed at her with the knife again, but Michelle didn't move this time as he closed in on her. With a blur of her hands, she grabbed his arm with the knife and broke it awkwardly, stabbing him in the neck with his own blade. With that she reached up to his throat and tore into the soft part under his chin. A sickening gurgle was echoed in the dank garage accompanied by a spray of blood as Michelle tore out the rest of his throat with her fingernails. His stunned eyes rolled to the side, but Michelle grabbed the back of his head and smashed it into the ground with a resounding crack that shattered his neck and skull. Another one rushed at her, and she rotated to the side so fast that he never saw her, then her long claws burst through his lower chest and eviscerated him! Upon the dingy pavement, his guts spilled out, and blood ran out like a waterfall, leaving a gaping hole out his back straight through along with a puddle of blood forming rapidly on the ground. He flopped slowly to the ground with a terrible splatter as more of his guts spilled out staining the ground. But as she walked past, Michelle stomped on the skull of the one she threw in the air before splattering his head across the ground with a fountain of blood and brains spraying one of the parked cars with gore. Her anger was now boiling over, and she began to walk toward the one she had hit with her arm first as he slowly got up still dazed. Michelle punched him so hard in the forehead she broke his spine and cracked his skull in one blow, and he bounced back first off the bloody concrete with another sickly crack echoing through the old garage. Just then the one with the gun showed himself and fired a round at her. Michelle heard the bullet whiz through the air, but she stepped to the side, dodging it easily with a mocking grin on her face and blood streaking her hands and arms. She grinned at him now, thinking she was going to shove that gun in his ass when she got closer to him.

In moments, Michelle began to move toward him so fast but got caught with a shot from another gun just as she was about to move in for another kill. The bullet hit her stomach and burned at first, and she fell to the ground, and now her chest burned a bit too. The shot hurt so bad not from the burns, just from the force of the blow and puncture. Dark blackened blood ran out of her chest as she grimaced, and wisps of smoke poured out too. She had to clear her head though; three were left. Then two of them closed in fast like they thought she was done. Just as they got closer, Michelle melted into the shadows and appeared behind the one who had shot her. She grabbed his hair from behind and effectively scalped him with a single slice of her wicked talonlike claws. He started to scream in agony as Michelle circled him angrily now.

"Oh, shut up!" she growled back and then, with her clawed hand, tore off his lower jaw!

Then she hurled it at the one who had missed her with the first shot. The impact hit him in the chest so hard with a spray of blood, and he doubled over. He tried to level the gun at her again, but Michelle was just too fast this time. She grabbed him by the throat and then screamed point-blank right in his face. His ears exploded with blood spraying as she dropped him to the ground, quite deaf and dazed as the hellish scream echoed through the musty garage, crack-

IN THE NAME OF SIN

ing the old pavement around him. She then watched as the thug who had his jaw ripped off stumbled past haplessly. Suddenly Michelle's massive claws struck the top of his head, crushing his skull through his spine with a sickly crack. The one left who had no hearing anymore tried to get up, but she kicked his legs out from under him, and he fell to a sitting position in the broken concrete. With an ominous laugh, Michelle walked behind him, and her clawed hands grabbed his head, and she began to squeeze hard. His eyes ruptured, and his nose had gray brain matter start to run out of it. Moments later, his skull crushed from the pressure with a resounding pop, showering the parking garage with more gore. But Michelle was so mad she tore what was left of his head clean off his shoulders and tossed it aside. She then kicked his lifeless body to the ground, spraying blood like a geyser upon one of the dirty support columns of the garage. She whirled around and then heard footsteps begin to run toward the stairs. Michelle took off after them mercilessly, grabbing her purse as she blurred by. She knew the score—no survivors, no witnesses, but in her eyes, her snack was just served.

The sound of sneakers pounding on the dirty pavement filled the lower level of a lonely Queens mall parking garage in the middle of the night. Michelle watched as whoever was running reached the stairs, but she grabbed their sweater and flung them at a parked car, shattering the windshield. She rushed over in a blur and pulled down their hood, and then Michelle got a shock; it was a girl. Her wicked smile became furious anger instantly, and she grabbed her by the front of her shirt with her still clawed hand.

"You were going to watch as they raped me! How could you, being a female yourself. You make me fucking sick, and I really hate humans at this moment!" she snarled, grabbing her hand and then forcing it through the already-broken windshield. The girl tried to scream, but Michelle grabbed her throat, cutting off the sound and her air momentarily. "Oh, don't you worry, you fucking bitch, you don't get to go as quick as your little buddies did, that I promise you. I was going to get gang-raped, how long do you think that was going to last? So, I'm returning the favor, you little shit. We're not done yet,

61

not by a long shot!" Michelle growled and then grabbed her hair and pulled her off the car, hurling her to the ground.

She dragged her toward the stairs, and the girl struggled to get free. Michelle tossed her roughly into the stairwell, and she tried to throw a punch at Michelle as she entered, but she caught her fist and then broke her hand easily with a twist and a sickly snap of bone. Michelle slammed the girl's head into the concrete wall, and with a rough push, Michelle knocked the girl back over and grabbed her foot as she began to ascend the stairs, dragging her behind.

"Please...lady...I didn't want to...but they forced me!" she pleaded to her, trying to get whatever this thing was to let her go.

But Michelle never looked back at her as she dragged her up the stairs. "I could care less about you and your excuses and, best yet, your disgusting life," she said back, kicking open the door at the top of the stairs.

With one hand and simple toss, she then hurled the girl through the air and out of the doorway to the rooftop parking lot. While she was on the ground, Michelle walked past but stomped hard on her foot, smashing it flat. The girl howled in pain, but Michelle grabbed her hair, pulling her up to meet her angry gaze.

"You better start being quieter, or I'm going to hurt you really bad. If you think this is pain, I assure you it's not. You're a piece of shit, and look at my jacket, it's ruined too. Do you know how much this costs?" Michelle hissed at her, slapping her across the face hard. Then she dumped the girl to the ground. "So, you were going to watch, and you know, I was raped a long time ago, and I was helpless back then. But you were going to watch me get humiliated again, left in pain and anguish—a lot like you are now. I should just let you live as a fucking cripple like you were going to let me live, but I'm not feeling very merciful tonight, kid," Michelle said, grabbing her bloody hand from the glass before and then began to drag her across the pavement.

The girl whimpered as the rough concrete tore through her clothes and skin. Once Michelle got close to the edge of the garage, she grabbed her throat again and hauled her up to meet her gaze once more. The girl looked like she had been put through hell and was barely even understanding what Michelle was saying right now.

IN THE NAME OF SIN

Between the fear in her eyes and the pain coursing through her body, it was too much for her mind right now.

"I hate most humans, but I think I hate you the most right now. So, I'm going to kill you nice and slow, unlike your fucking friends." Michelle snarled and shook her roughly, only to terrorize her even further.

With that, Michelle's jaw shook and popped, and her tongue slipped past her lips and split in front of the girl's eyes. Her sharp thorn cut the girl's cheek that was still in her grasp and then sliced down her throat, drawing blood as it passed over her skin. The girl cried out in pain and fear once more, but it didn't seem to help. Michelle then drove her thorn deeply into her chest, piercing her heart, and the poor girl began to whimper, feeling the sharp thorn dig through her flesh and into her heart slowly. The two barbed fangs on the ends of her split tongue latched into her skin hard, embedding, delivering a horrible numbing anesthetic. Michelle began to feed, feeling her thorn had found her victim's essence, her rich life force. The girl's skin began pulsating as Michelle tapped directly into her soul's very essence. Michelle then began to feast on the girl stealing as much essence as she could, but just as she was about to devour her soul, and just as it began to tear free, she stopped. Michelle tore her bloody thorn loose with a twist, and it retracted into her mouth as coagulated blood from her feeding deeply upon the girl oozed from the wound in her chest. This battered and broken girl was barely conscious now, but Michelle hardly cared either.

"Not that easy, you bitch, you don't die that simple." With that, Michelle shoved her bloodied broken body off the parking garage and down onto the street below. "Say hello to your friends in hell," Michelle yelled after her as she fell to the street below.

Seconds later, a sickening thud accompanied her hitting the pavement below, and Michelle walked toward the doorway to go get her car before the police arrived. For the first time, she winced, and she grabbed her lower chest, and dark blood ran through her fingers. The drops left wisps of smoke as they fell behind her heading for the door. Michelle got from her bag her keys for the Ferrari and never even thought of the carnage she had left behind tonight either.

63

CHAPTER 9

The cool night air back in Manhattan felt much better on her skin than that horrible dirty parking garage did in Queens. But still the pain in her stomach wasn't helping either. A little while ago, Michelle had parked her Ferrari over in Midtown East at a self-parking garage. The dark windows of her car would keep out prying eyes for at least a day. She had bled a decent amount in the car as she sped out of Queens, so her dark-black blood was all over the seats, leaving behind stains as it became ashes. She was forcing her body to heal slowly due to how much essence she had used in the two fights, let alone the all-night search for Tony. Essence or life force is found in the blood since the heart is the cradle of the soul; remnants of the soul are found in the blood throughout the body, and that's what Immortals fed upon with their thorn; the blood meant very little but was still quite sweet. This was the reason only fresh or living human blood would work; collected blood was without essence because it dissipated quickly when separated from the soul. Immortals didn't drink the blood, they siphoned it, separating the essence from the blood using their thorn and a unique organ below it called the *terot*. So as an Immortal fed, the blood was stripped of its life force; and if enough was taken, death would soon follow. Allowing her body to heal rapidly could end up in a poor situation right now. Essence was important to heal and power her abilities but also maintain her immortality, and a victim's soul was easy enough to consume while feeding. The act of consuming a soul had consequences of its own; it was always the best way to get the most essence possible, but by doing so, it brought unspeakable pleasure for an Immortal and made it easier to fall victim to that unnatural hunger again. The more souls she consumed, the worse her humanity was ruined, because it harmed her own tattered soul in the process. Right now, Michelle was trying to preserve what she had left. Once that was gone, her will would fail utterly, then the demonic side of her had won in the end, allowing the demon to become part of her soul, and the two of them would become one, damning her forever.

What was once her human side would cease to control her body entirely. Hence, the demon was out of its cage for good, and her conscience was placed in it forever. An Immortal's body was like two halves of the same person: the demon and the soul. Currently Michelle was what was referred to as a "willful possession," and her body still housed her soul, but it also housed a powerful demon that was using it to hide. Most times the demon was willing to help as long as it got fed essence, but when she was in the situation like she was in now, it got agitated. When wounded, essence was used to heal, but that same essence was used to fuel her abilities and immortality. She had used a lot in the fights and the entire night's escapades. When Michelle was shot, she was functioning on pure anger and hatred or rage, easy enough for a demon to do in the moment. Raging was when she allowed the demon in her body to come close to the surface and aid her usually through immense anger that resulted in her evil nature to take control, giving her a taste of what it was like if they became one. But now she had a real problem; there was still a bullet in her, and Michelle hadn't taken enough essence from the girl and opted to toss her off the roof instead, still lucid, in that evil rage. But in retrospect, that was a poor decision; at least taking enough essence to kill her would've refreshed her. The little essence she had taken helped, but taking her soul would've healed her fully and refueled her body completely but scared Michelle's soul yet again.

Now Michelle was desperate to feed once more, and that was the reason she wasn't healing fast. It could result in another rampage like before, but this time her demon would be calling the shots, not her. When the demon hunted without help from her, it was like turning loose a beast to do what it wished to whomever crossed its path, mortal or Immortal. With her will and conscience there to hold the demon at bay, at least she was in charge. Without her soul in the way, she wouldn't be picky on who she fed on then and where that was too. Another risk she wasn't willing to take right now either. It almost always resulted with consuming an entire soul's essence, maybe even a few—scaring her own soul badly in the process, and that had its own mental repercussions too because she would have to live with the horrid memories afterward. Michelle would get to watch as her demon tormented her by ruthlessly killing anything it could find for the pure pleasure of it. Those memories always stayed with you and never allowed you to forget the demon lurking inside you, just beneath the flesh, a horrible killing machine with little regard for any life. Going to the club was out, she was a wreck; and if someone spotted her and put two and two together, she'd have to admit to the slaughterhouse in Queens. Elijah was already mad enough at her over the first fight.

Mistress Anneke wouldn't care about seven humans dying violently, but Michelle had left all the bodies to be found easily enough. That fact alone would anger Anneke due to the fact that her actions threatened all the Immortals of New York with a stunt like that, not to mention her house too. Michelle had also been shadow-walking from place to place trying to get to her flat in SoHo, but she was finding it difficult now because her essence was fading. When that happened, going ravenous wasn't far behind, and then the real carnage would begin. She leaned back against a cool wall, and her body demanded sustenance now; her chest began to hurt, and as it got worse, it was her demon breaking through. She was getting dangerously close to losing herself as the agony continued. A ravenous Immortal was dangerous beyond words, and most time the carnage left in its wake was unspeakable. When an Immortal spoke of being ravenous, it was at the point when their demon was about to break its cage and rampage; this is when the demon would have more power than her mind and will. Her mind would go in a cage for a bit and

IN THE NAME OF SIN

let the true nature of a demon run free in the city as she watched. But worse yet, the more times an Immortal became ravenous and gave in and allowed the demon to feed on its own because of lack of will, the easier it would happen again! Michelle realized she couldn't be picky anymore and needed to feed now; she was getting too close. Soon it would end in slaughter and maybe something she couldn't cover up this time or maybe something utterly unspeakable, so she had to feed.

From a dark alleyway, Michelle had been watching a pimp beating his girls for a little bit now. Killing him only helped the girls in her eyes, so Michelle had chosen her next victim. She was just waiting for the right moment, and this is why most Immortals hated "street hunting" alone because she had to be very careful. Just then the last of the girls left, and Michelle ducked into another shadow and appeared behind the large man. She grabbed him by the shoulder and dragged him through another shadow with her and appeared on the rooftop above. No words were said as Michelle fell on him and drove her thorn deep into his chest, splitting his aorta open, tapping into his essence; and her fangs latched in. Savagely she had begun to feed, driving her thorn in deep; there was no subtlety about this. The anesthetic was just taking affect, but the large man grabbed her throat, and in response, Michelle grabbed his arm and twisted it hard. The bones snapped, and a cracking noise followed, rendering it useless. The pimp did his best to let out a half-hearted screamed, but the numbing anesthetic took effect. But Michelle punched him hard into the jaw, shattering it, as her heart reversed, and she began to feed quickly. In moments, Michelle had nearly devoured his soul as she fed viciously from this man's body; she felt her heart reverse, and in moments, it was over—the pimp was dead. She ripped her thorn free, letting out a long sigh, but turned the dead pimp's head to face hers, and his eyes weren't drained and white. The eyes were the windows to the soul; if she had taken his, then the eyes would've been stark white or without irises. Michelle breathed out a sigh of relief that her soul was not harmed yet again. Her thorn had just settled to her throat once more as she stood up and her jaw relocated too. She then used the sleeve of her ruined jacket to wipe her mouth clean.

Just then something hit the ground, and Michelle picked it up. It was the slug from before that had been buried in her lower chest. Her body was healed, and it had expelled the slug in the process. Next was taking care of the corpse, and for that, Michelle knelt down and, with a few rough blows, smashed the pimp's skull through part of the concrete rooftop. She then grabbed a large concrete block, dropping it in on top of the crushed head of her victim. It now looked like murder and covered up the fact Michelle had nearly consumed his soul. With that she walked through another shadow toward SoHo again. But the problem was, it was getting early, and getting there was starting to become a bigger problem.

Over in East Village, Elijah had just gotten home an hour or so ago. He wasn't happy with Michelle at the moment, who had vanished again at the club after the fight in the Abyss. He would want an explanation for this time for sure. He sat back for a moment to relax because the sun would be up soon. It was almost time for him to call it a day. Sunlight was lethal to an elder since they were reborn in darkness, and it was extremely painful even in small doses, unlike lessers or thralls, who weren't so hindered. Thralls were unaffected, and lessers had to stay out of the zenith of sun at midday only, so it was best for an elder to sleep to avoid it. Just then, there was knock at his door, and Elijah set down his wineglass with a rough thump. Whoever this was better have a damn good reason for bothering him right now, he thought as he stormed toward his front door. When he opened it, he got the shock of his life; his prodigy looked like she had gone through a war! He hurried her inside because dawn was so close. Once he locked the door again, he turned toward Michelle, who looked disheveled right now.

"This better be good, Michelle, you look like shit, and you smell horrible too. Need I ask what's going on?" he said, walking past her, annoyed seeing the state she was in.

Michelle took off her ruined jacket and sat down on the tile floor so as not to stain anything. Elijah loved the color white for this house's decor here in the East Village, one of his many properties. He enjoyed themes for most of the places he owned, and this one was a white decor that he had paid a very famous New York interior designer to create for him a few years ago. She had to be careful—everything was white, and everything was very expensive too.

"I had a small patch of bad luck tonight, and it got way out of hand over in Queens," she said back, rubbing her healed chest still sore from the gunshot.

Elijah picked up his glass and sighed for a moment. "So that ruckus in the news in Queens was your doing earlier. Why am I not surprised after you tore out poor Iris's thorn? But really, Michelle, seven bodies piled up at the morgue and some news stations are saying it looks like a wild animal tore them to shreds. Luckily, they think it's gang related now. But did you have to toss someone off the damn roof!" he asked, carefully taking a sip of his glass of red wine on the perfect white couch as he sat back and relaxed again.

But Michelle scowled back at him then. "They were going to fucking rape me, Elijah!" she snapped back. "So I fucking killed them all, and you know what, the one I tossed off the roof was a girl who was in on it. Sound like a familiar story, huh?"

Elijah drained his glass and set it down again; he knew the story all too well. "Still, Michelle, did it have to be a rampage like that? If Anneke finds out it was you, she's going to be sore with you. Why were you in Queens in the first place anyway, of all places?" he asked her, a bit surprised.

Michelle stood up and then let her anger go. "I was looking for Tony…I kind of…like him. But I got jumped looking for him at his job at the mall, of all places. I got shot and had to come here. Right now, I can't make it to my place, and I had to ditch my car in Midtown East in a self-park garage because it has to be cleaned. There was way too much blood and ash in it to take it back to our garage right now, so I figured further the better. Then I had to heal up, so that took time too. I ended up having to street hunt solo, you know, the old way. So, you can add another body to the list too if you like. You think I wanted to come here after what happened at the Abyss? You took that Bael bitch's side. She started with your prodigy, and you took her side, but I was kind of desperate right now, so here I am. Oh, the irony, right?" she said back to him as calmly as she could give the situation.

"Well, at least you hid the car, fed, and avoided the club too, so I don't think Anneke wants to hear this story either. Go freshen up, and you can use the guest suite for the day. You were smart, Michelle, you covered your tracks the best you could and kept this as quiet as possible. But in order to heal Iris, we had to use almost all of the club's supply of Syn-Es.9, so you're going to replace that. Iris, on the other hand, will have to pay for the damages to the Abyss because, yes, she started that altercation," he said back to her, frowning a bit because Michelle made a retching face at the mere mention of Synthetic Essence, or Syn-Es.9. "So, what's your plan with this Tony though? I'm only asking because you risked much to find him. But I did find him quite an improvement over a few of your choices lately when it comes to humans. Our meeting was brief, but you know me as a judge of character most times," Elijah said as he finished his glass and put the stopper in the crystal decanter for the wine on the table.

Michelle stopped pacing and then thought for a moment. "I'm intrigued, Elijah, but as for my intentions, well, I have no intentions of letting the world of humans have him again, that's for damn sure. As for your judge of character, I've never known you to get that wrong either," she said back, taking another step.

"A possible prodigy perhaps then?" he asked with a raised brow and standing up himself.

Suddenly Michelle stopped her angry pacing and then thought about that prospect again. It had come to her a few times, and maybe it was time to seriously entertain those thoughts, even with her disastrous history in that department.

"Perhaps, Elijah, perhaps, but I must dwell on it more. I like the human, but eternity, I would have to be certain," she said back, quickening her step for a moment.

"Until you've decided, consider him still off-limits to other Immortals at the club for now. I shall spread the word tonight the human belongs to you still," he said as Michelle began to head to the guest suite of the house.

She reached the en suite door in the guest room, and she grinned slightly. She liked the sound of that at this very moment. But in her heart, she liked the idea of a prodigy of her own that much more, she

IN THE NAME OF SIN

was now seriously considering Tony to become her companion for all eternity—especially if Elijah had seen something in him to mention such a thing; he was always a good judge of character.

Hours later, the sun was still up over the city of Manhattan, but that didn't stop Michelle's phone from ringing. She was slumbering in her underwear, the only clothes she had not ruined by last night's rampage. She was still very sleepy in Elijah's guest suite when it shook her from her slumber. She reached over with groggy hands, and she didn't belong awake right now. She grabbed the phone on its fourth ring and looked at a number she didn't know. She almost tossed the phone into the pile of ruined, bloody clothes on the floor next to the bed but decided to pick it up anyway. She said a very weak hello as she tried to stay awake right now. Her body demanded rest, and she was fighting it. An Immortal elder didn't belong awake during the day; just then, it was the voice she had been yearning for, for two days that called to her softly.

"Michelle, I couldn't wait till dark to call you. I know you're sleeping, but like I said, I couldn't wait. I needed…to hear your voice," he said sweetly, and to her, it was everything she needed right now.

Michelle rolled onto her back and then smiled weakly because deep in her heart, this is what she wanted too. "It's okay, sugar, I can fall back to sleep in a New York minute. Where have you been though?" she asked, knowing the answer already.

"Upstate. It seems my beeper didn't work up there too well, but I had to stay another day. We made the finals, and the kids were all excited," Tony said back happily.

She took a deep breath trying to stay awake, but her eyes were closing fast. "That's fine, and I'm happy for you, and I've missed you too, and yes, I'd like it very much to see you soon," she said back, still fading but fighting to stay awake.

"I won't keep you from your rest. I just wanted to know if I could come and see you tonight?" he asked her, and she smiled a little wider with her eyes still closing.

"Of course, you can, always come to me when you want," she said, almost falling asleep but willing herself to stay awake. "Call me later, Tony, and I will send a car for you, no more trains. You get driven to me from now on," she said back, still very groggy now.

He agreed and told her he would let her get back to sleep. She listened to the line click, and she let the phone fall to the floor. Sleep was taking her again fast, but as she drifted away, her decision was made. Tony was to become hers for eternity. She had chosen her prodigy, and Tony would join her as a fellow Immortal elder and, with a little luck, her mate. She smiled once more and drifted away with the thought that her loneliness was about to end. He would join her, or this time, she was going to die too; there was no going back for either of them this time. Michelle didn't want to live on without him; she was tired of this life of loneliness. Sleep finally took her, and around her closed eyes, small bluish-red flames began to emanate once more, the sure sign of an Immortal elder. As Michelle slept, her demon was wide awake and now watched over her.

CHAPTER 10

The night finally chased away the day's light, and Michelle Du'Pree, with the final setting of the sun, opened her eyes and sat up. She was still in Elijah's guest suite and shook her hair out of her face. She saw her phone on the floor where she had tossed it, and it wasn't her imagination he had called. Her heart skipped yet another beat as she began to get up. She gathered the ruined clothes and placed them into a plastic bag to be incinerated due to how much blood was all over them. Michelle's split tongue began to twitch a little, a sure sign she had to feed before Tony arrived. Tonight would be her first of three nights with him.

In order to create another elder, Michelle needed to feed on him three nights in a row before the stroke of midnight of each night. She had to first taste his essence then sup upon his life and finally experience his soul. All this had to be done without killing him, so the third would be the most difficult because it was very tempting. He would then be surrounded in a pale-red aura that only she would be able to see and sense that marked him as her chosen. But her own lust would inverse on her, making him so alluring to her, and she had to keep her composure afterward. Next, she had three nights to deliver the fourth and final time she needed to feed upon him and was even more difficult than the third time. She had to feed from him, but he also had to feed from her too. They needed to do so until the point that both their essence and souls had mixed fully. This would trigger Michelle's dark gift to be granted to her chosen, thus creating a new elder, but the difficult part was they couldn't spill a drop of blood either of them; they needed all of it to create. This is where Michelle had failed in the past recently. This all had to be done before the start of a new night, but the worst part was if she failed again, she could only save herself by devouring his soul, or she would die too. Michelle had already decided this was her last attempt at creating a prodigy, and she would rather die with him than destroy him utterly.

She finished with cleaning up the guest room as she thought out her next nights with him, but first she needed to speak to Elijah, her creator. She then decided that she would let Tony recover from her feedings until the last and final night, then they would both face death together. Michelle was certain that the world of humans would destroy him one day, and better for him to walk in the darkness with the Immortals and her especially than allow that to happen. Michelle then heard a knock at the door, and when she opened it, a package wrapped in brown paper was in the hall. She picked it opening the package and found a simple pair of sweatpants, T-shirt, and sweater. She took them out and dressed fast so she could get back to her place to get cleaned up and changed. She had to get ready for her guest who was leaving the world of light very soon. When she walked downstairs, she found Elijah in the kitchen, and he was already dressed for the club. He handed her a paper cup with a plastic lid to take her coffee with her. Michelle saw it and rumpled her nose in disgust.

"Have you decided about your mortal friend, or should I expect more carnage tonight?" Elijah asked her humorously in attempt to get Michelle in a better mood from last night.

She took the cup and frowned; she hated paper cups and especially plastic sipping lids. Good coffee deserved a proper cup made of glass or pottery to drink it from—not this crap; it felt like it came from a gas station. She took a sip, and luckily the coffee was quite good. She expected as much. Elijah knew how to make what she liked, being her creator—dark French roast with two teaspoons of sugar. After her first sip and taking a moment to let the caffeine do its work, she answered him with a smile finally.

"Yes, I have. He's joining me in immortality, and he will become my prodigy. Elijah, I ask you as my creator, may I take this human and make him into an Immortal elder? He shall join House Du'Pree as one of its elders and sons. His station in the house will be that of our sovereign, and he shall stand with us and direct the way our house shall dictate the future of New York. I will be responsible for him, and his sins will be mine to bear. I ask you as my creator to show me the respect and allow my choice to be given your blessing."

Elijah raised a brow and took another drink from his cup. Michelle knew how to ask, and the Tradition of Creation had begun. It was up to the creator to say if she could bestow her dark gift on him, and an elder could only do this just once in their entire lives: create an equal companion, so the choice was critical as well as difficult. He took a few steps and then turned slowly to face her.

"You understand what you ask, correct? You risk his life because while he is mortal, nothing is certain. Are you ready to bear the consequences if you succeed or fail? You hold in your body the future of your house, are you prepared to do what you might have to in order to survive?" he asked her very seriously, and Michelle realized this was just part of the tradition.

Michelle looked him in the eyes and then answered in a very serious tone, "My soul is prepared to see this through, and I ask again, may I take him as my own for all eternity, as my companion?" she answered in the traditional way.

Elijah then thought for a moment, and he had the right to refuse her or make her wait for his answer. But after meeting the mortal, he felt he had value, but still he was concerned. "Yes, my prodigy, my permission is granted, and I shall be his overseer. I will judge his sins and punish you both if I must. Go take what is now rightfully yours," he said back, thinking this was Michelle's best choice she had ever made when it came to prodigy material in his eyes. As much as he was concerned, he had to allow this because the house needed to grow to survive.

Michelle grinned back that the tradition was complete; permission was asked and given. Mistress Anneke would never accept him into her house if she had not asked, as the traditions commanded. She would order him destroyed, and as matron of the house, it was within her rights. Worse yet, Michelle would have to do it though in order to take back her dark gift.

A little while later, Michelle left Elijah's townhouse, and he surprised her because her Ferrari had been cleaned and waiting for her, and she drove back to her SoHo flat to prepare. She had to feed first and then prepare for Tony's arrival later tonight. When she walked in, her phone rang, and she picked it up. It was Tony, and he apologized for calling her this afternoon. Michelle assured him he was allowed to call whenever he liked. She told him she was getting ready for tonight and would send a car in hour or so to get him. He was to be brought directly to her. He had gone from being just another mortal to her soon-to-be chosen because of the tradition she evoked. No one would dare harm him now anywhere in the city very soon. When a mortal was chosen, he became off-limits under any circumstances to any other Immortal except the one that had called for the Tradition of Creation, which Michelle had done with her creator. Now he was to be treated as one of them, because he would be very soon. But she was so looking forward to seeing him again tonight, so after they hung up, she hurried inside to get ready. She had to get to the Factory first so she could be well-fed when he arrived. After Michelle had hung up with him, she called a car service and sent them to his address to pick him up and made sure they understood he was a VIP tonight at the club and a friend of the Du'Pree family. She then got in the shower and let the hot water clean away the rest of last night. She needed to dress extraordinary tonight, and that always took time too. But Tony seemed to like her rebellious side, and she decided to dress to please him, and then she got a very clever idea to get her first feeding. She checked her watch, and she had plenty of time; the first had to be done before the stroke of midnight.

*****

IN THE NAME OF SIN

When Michelle arrived at the club as quickly as she could, she was asked by one of the attendants to see Elijah before she got comfortable. She usually knew this meant problems, and if that was the case, it was usually something for the house too. She was supposed to meet Tony in a few hours, and right now she didn't want these distractions at the moment, not to mention she needed to feed. It was early enough, and the sun had barely set, but House Du'Pree was an important part of Michelle's life. It provided her the protection, money, and prestige she enjoyed in the city. She took the stairs down to the Abyss, and once inside, she headed for the bar but walked past it and then around it to the right. This appeared to be a simple storage area, but when Michelle got to the back, she pulled a hidden handle between two boxes of scotch. The wall slid away, and she took the hidden elevator to the secret fifth floor of the building. Once she got off the elevator, she turned to the right and headed toward the end of the hall that was very much in need of a renovation because it looked like a throwback to the 1970s. She walked through the heavy wooden door at the end of the hallway, and Elijah was behind his old desk in the office here. He had the safe up here open, and that kept valuables and petty cash here too. He motioned to the chair in front of the desk as he glanced over a few pieces of paper furiously and hardly looked up either. Elijah was the brains behind a lot of House Du'Pree's prominence, and if he was this interested in something, then he had a very good reason. But if he had the safe opened up here, there was something very interesting going on. No wonder Cassie was busy before when she called her; now Michelle was wondering what was up.

"You know, Elijah, I care for you a lot, but I have quite a night planned, so if you can speed this up, it would help. I've got a guest tonight that I'd like to make sure we have quite a time tonight. You do remember what I just asked you earlier, right?" Michelle said to him, and Elijah looked up from what he was reading, annoyed at the moment.

He set the paper aside and then folded his hands in front of him, another bad sign that Michelle wasn't going to like what was coming next. "Then I'll make this quick for you. Anneke has asked to speak to you tonight, and I'm obliged to tell you, is all. Now I hope you set aside some time before your guest is due to arrive because she insisted too, Michelle," Elijah said sternly, and now Michele looked like she was about to have a fit.

"Goddamnit, Elijah, it takes time to get to the Du'Pree Estate! I'll never get back here before my guest arrives. I just can't, not tonight!" Michelle said back with a scowl but was secretly worried Anneke had put two and two together about the carnage in Queens or was angry about the fight in the Abyss last night.

"Not at the Estate, Michelle, here in the city, and tonight too, she insisted. Anneke is here and has asked for you to drop by her place over in Murray Hill and chat. Now it's not far from here, so if you leave soon, you'll be back with plenty of time to spare. I would go and see what she wishes. Is she not the matron of our house?" Elijah said back to her and then picked up another folder and began to look through it.

But Michelle was shocked that Anneke was in the city at the moment; she normally spent most of her time in the Estate. For some reason unknown, since the 1940s, Anneke preferred the solitude of her massive estate grounds in Cold Spring Harbor. But she was also a Succubus that was centuries old; no one really knew how old, but Elijah knew, and he would never tell. Being what she was, she needed essence just like Michelle did, so Anneke had a very posh townhouse apartment in Murray Hill, which was the place she goes when she was on the prowl. Most times Anneke went there alone and without warning either; she preferred to hunt in the middle of the upper society of Manhattan's elite, a snob hunting other snobs. When Anneke did such a thing, she used her apartment to do so. If she was getting ready to head out to hunt, then she would be inclined to be hospitable. Anneke was no different than Michelle; she needed lust-filled essence, and the best way to achieve that was sex, plain and simple.

"Fine, fine, at least it's not a damn trip to the North Shore of Long-fucking-Island. I'll head there after this, and hopefully it's short and sweet too. You know how much I just love to speak for extended time with Anneke, of all people," Michelle said back to him and began to get up, still upset but happy she would be back at the club fast too.

"Behave, Michelle, and if I know her, she's interested in your guest as much as you are. I did tell her you invoked the tradition, so she's interested but at the same time curious too. Show her the proper respect I know you can. She is concerned about our bloodline, is all. But if I know her, if she's in Murray Hill, she'll be quick. This is why I always tell you to be mindful of what you do some nights. You never know when she could be here. Imagine last night's festivities went on and she was in the city. I'm thinking she's going to want an explanation, and if you're wondering, I haven't said a single word to her about either the fight in the club nor the ruckus in Queens," Elijah replied and then flipped open a folder and snatched a gold pen off the desk.

"Well, it is her little hideaway when she wants to embrace the Succubus side of her life, instead of being a reclusive snob and absentee queen of the Manhattan socialites. But hey, we all get horny from time to time, right?" Michelle snapped back, heading for the door again.

Elijah looked up again and tapped the pen on the desk slowly. "One night, my young prodigy, you will test your luck too far with her, and it will be a sorry moment for you. Now go and see her. I know what she's up to as well, and yes, I would suspect it will be brief if she's in the mood."

Michelle left the office and headed quickly for the elevator again. She wanted to get to Murray Hill and speak with Anneke and then head right back here before Tony arrived. With a little luck, the time to travel there would be longer than the actual conversation. It was no secret that Michelle and Anneke had been at odds for more than a century, and not much was going to change that any time soon after what she had done to her so long ago.

The trip to Murray Hill was short, and Michelle checked her watch just as she stepped out the car in her long leather coat covering her outfit for the night. She had a little more than an hour till Tony arrived, and she had to hope Anneke wasn't in one of her chatty moods. If she was one thing, it was unpredictable, to put it lightly; and some nights, she still found ways to surprise Michelle even though she knew her for so long. She walked up the beautiful steps to one of the nicest townhouses in all of Murray Hill and hit the only buzzer on the door. The townhouse could easily have two to three occupants, but Anneke owned the entire place. Michelle tapped her foot impatiently as she waited for an answer, and soon a man's voice answered she knew and never liked either. It was Harden, the only servant that was allowed here. Anneke had a butler here that saw to the townhouse and happened to be one of her lessers too. A mortal that had been turned by an elder that was linked to them. He saw to Anneke's needs here when she stayed, but Michelle liked to needle him about. Anneke always needed someone to take out her trash, and no one did that better than Harden did.

"Let me in, Harden, I'm here to see my mother," Michelle said and nearly gagged saying that too as she adjusted her long coat. She really didn't need Anneke seeing the special surprise she had on for Tony; she was an aristocrat and a proud snob—she would never approve.

A moment passed, and there was no answer, just the lock buzzing, and Michelle grabbed the door handle and headed inside. Harden was annoying but no fool either; she was an elder of House Du'Pree and its current consort too. Anneke would toss him from the rooftops if he dared to say or do something to stop her. With him never saying a word meant Anneke expected her, and she walked down the short hallway, and the front door was open. When she headed inside, Harden shut the door and asked for her coat, but she declined. He was a tall man with tightly cropped brown hair and hazel eyes too. He walked quickly away from Michelle without a word. The last time she had spoken to him, there were words said, and Anneke slapped him across the foyer with a single blow. He still looked at her like he wanted to finish the argument but wasn't willing to risk his life either. Harden knew Michelle's reputation too; if she wanted to, he would be dead before he got out two words. Anneke would be more upset about the mess left in her townhouse than Harden being dead. The huge apartment was decorated in Art Deco fashion reminiscent of the late 1980s—light color tones, sharp angles, and gold or silver accents. Michelle walked up the winding stairs to the third floor and headed into the grand lounge there. She walked down the five steps into the sunken living room and headed right for the bar, only to pick up the bottle of wine that was open and then took a glass from the gold hanging rack. She poured for herself, but in moments, Anneke walked down the same stairs and saw that and frowned.

"Harden! Why is my daughter pouring *herself* a glass of wine and you're not doing it! I find it distasteful that she's doing the job of a servant. Get in here this instant and remedy the situation!" Anneke said loudly and took a seat on the white couches in her long black evening gown with a frown on her red lips.

"Good evening to you too, Anneke," Michelle said with a scowl of her own as Harden walked in and poured a glass of wine for Anneke.

He handed her the glass, and Anneke took it by the stem and then shooed him away with a few motions of her black-gloved hand. This was the gorgeous woman who controlled most of the city, and she was not only one of the richest women in the state but also the country. Unknown to everyone else, Anneke Elisabeth Du'Pree was a vastly powerful Succubus that had been alive for who knew how long. She was one person everyone wanted to talk to in the city, but if they knew better, they would stay away. Nothing was for free when you dealt with Anneke; everything had a price, and sometimes it was your life. Once Harden was gone, Anneke motioned to Michelle to take a seat on a love seat across from her, and she walked over still hoping this would be over with fast; she truly hated being in a room alone with this woman.

"Well, you called, Anneke, and as much as I have my own plans tonight, I came, so what do you need of me?" Michelle said to her, setting her glass on the brass and frosted glass coffee table.

"Michelle, stop. Is it too difficult for me to wish to speak to my daughter while I'm in the city? I still see you as such. Would it be so hard for you to address me as *Mother* again like you did so long ago?" Anneke said back and then took a gentle sip of her glass like the snob she was known for then grinned again evilly.

Her long honey-blond hair was down tonight and styled, and it was obvious she was preparing to leave soon. But Anneke was a beauty to behold, the face of an angel, with old-Hollywood beauty too. She had the green eyes of a great hunting cat and such a way with her along with her melodic voice that lulled the unwary into a false sense of security. Her unearthly beauty only hid the secret that she was evil to the core, and Michelle was certain her humanity faded long ago. Anneke Du'Pree was not a person you underestimated in the least; the ones who did were either very sorry or very dead.

"It's been a long time since I called you that, and I don't see that changing anytime soon. I said I'd be cordial, Anneke, and I am. Now what did you call me here for, so you can get to whatever you have planned and I can get back to my plans. As for me calling you *Mother* again in public, I get it, we need to keep up appearances, but in private and among our own kind, I would think a first-name basis is the best we will ever get to," Michelle said back to her and then took a fast sip of her glass, once more trying to be brief.

"Very well, Michelle," Anneke said to her, setting her glass down, annoyed. "I asked you here about your newest little friend. According to Elijah, you seem quite fond of him—very fond, I must say, to invoke the Tradition of Creation. I was wondering what has gotten your interests in the first place though? Tell me a little about him. You do realize that you cannot hold the bloodline of our house forever. In order for our great house to gain strength, we need to grow and prosper. I've been hoping that you might have found a suitable mortal soon. According to Elijah, you seem to be as fond of him as you were that young man in Paris so long ago. So, when will you begin to finally help our house to grow?" Anneke asked her and then sat back, placing both her arms across the top of the couch behind her.

Michelle now grinned back hearing that; she knew this was no social call. Anneke was wondering about Tony; she wanted to know what had made her select him. As much as she felt Tony was more than worthy, she had asked for permission and invoked the tradition, but still nothing was for certain either. *Let Anneke wait until I'm successful enough to make the final attempt. Let her wait and see if I'm able*

IN THE NAME OF SIN

to do what I still feel would never happen or let her weep finally when her house is destroyed because this is my last attempt too. If I fail, this time I'm more than willing to die with Tony instead of taking his soul.

"Give me time and let me see how this one plays out, Anneke, I don't wish to pressure myself or give you false hope either. My last few attempts were failures, and you know how easy it is to create. Maybe this time I will be successful and maybe not. I will tell you that he is quite worthy, and I have a strong feeling about this one," Michelle said back to her with a sly grin.

Anneke nodded to her but secretly hoped she had found what she felt was her perfect match. A long time ago, Anneke had a feeling about Michelle, and she knew that her prodigy would be the key to greatness of her house. But after two failed attempts, she had learned nothing was for certain, and all she could do was wait and see how this played out. Michelle was a valuable part of this house, more than she even knew, but it was her prodigy that would complete her. For now, Michelle was in good spirits, and that was an improvement over her normally snide attitude and destructive behavior.

"Now, Michelle, be mindful and most of all careful around mortals, even with ones you think have quality. We must always be wary. Immortals and humans are a poor mix most times. They're prey, and we're the predator," Anneke said, and just then, the doorbell rang, and she smiled widely. "Ah, my date for the evening, Jonas McQuillan. We're heading to Fifth Avenue and trying out that new Moroccan restaurant that the papers are raving about. If you like, you and of course your new friend could accompany us. I'd love to meet him and see his quality firsthand," Anneke said to her and stood up but looked back fast. "Oh, when you get a chance, could you please see to that asset we have in the mayor's office soon? You've been busy, and I didn't think it was relevant before, but he's becoming an issue. If he doesn't see things our way, then remove him, Michelle, you know how. Loose ends like that could be a small disaster for us."

Michelle nodded back and then drained her glass fast. "Thank you, Anneke, but no, thank you, we have reservations downtown and might decide that privacy is in order just like you'll need as well by the end of the night, I'm sure. As for the mayor's office, I will see to it. Mason has been under my little spell for some time, but I think he just misses his Trisha. I'll use my illusions soon enough and give him a little visit," Michelle replied and walked with her from the lounge. She knew that Anneke wished to take up the guise of the girl Mason thought she was and make him see reason; if not, then he was going to have a little accident.

But Michelle also knew just what Anneke was up to tonight too. This man was about to find out just how dangerous Anneke Du'Pree could be. They would head out for drinks and dinner, and Anneke would begin to spin lust around him throughout it. Later on, they would come back here, and they would make love or so, this Jonas would think. Anneke would use sex to cultivate the lust and then begin to feed. She was a bit sadistic when she did this because she enjoyed bringing her lover for the night close to death and then let him recover, only to begin again later. She would feast from him three to five times and soon begin to not only drink down his essence but also shorten his life span due to the damages to his body. Michelle never did that; she fed and either killed or didn't; and when she did kill, it was swift. Anneke had hardly changed at all when it came to her tendencies over the years. Where Michelle felt horrible sometimes over the things she had done, Anneke never did. This was what Michelle had meant when Harden was the best at getting rid of Anneke's trash. He would be the one to clean up after Anneke took the soul of her lover for the night by removing the body. How many of Anneke's sexual partners had died in this house, was the thought that slipped into Michelle's head as they walked from the lounge and to the stairs. All she could think was she couldn't leave fast enough. Meanwhile, Anneke was a bit upset to hear Michelle was still bitter with her. She truly missed her company some nights and longed for those nights in Paris when she took time to feast with her daughters. Oh, the nights they had; hopefully sooner or later the house would grow once more. All that was left was to wait and see. But Anneke could wait—she had for hundreds of years. But if Michelle was being this secretive about her new friend, there was quality in the young man—that, she was certain of.

CHAPTER 11

The neighborhood in Queens around Tony's small house was abuzz with the long black limousine that was waiting outside his house. He had seen the car and shook his head. *Did she have to send a limo?* he began to think. But that was Michelle, everything had to be just right in her eyes. He was just hoping that not everyone had seen this huge black car waiting outside his house. Tony then decided he might as well get this over with. He hoped, by moving as fast as he could, he could get to the car before his neighbors came out to check it out. He walked out of his front door quickly and saw his sister walking down the sidewalk, and he hurried up. Tony opened the door and got in just as Marissa walked up and started to walk into the house, looking back more than once. He let out a slow sigh of relief and thanked God for tinted windows. A moment later, the car pulled away from his house. The privacy glass slid down a bit, and the driver told him that Ms. Du'Pree had some chilled Cristal Champagne ready for him to enjoy and left a small gift in the envelope next to the bottle. He poured a glass and then took a sip, but when he opened the envelope, his jaw nearly hit the floor. It was a check from the new city beautification program that the Du'Pree family had funded for a half a million dollars! The check was made out to the martial arts academy he trained at for the amazing job they had done at the tournament. This would keep the academy open for years to come and have enough to update the entire place, all the while having money to spare. He couldn't wait to give this to them. Underneath her crazy club girl persona, Michelle Du'Pree had a heart of gold, or so he thought. In reality, it was to be his parting gift to the world of humans in her eyes.

Meanwhile in Chelsea, Michelle had arrived moments ago from Murray Hill. She was just about to head up and hunt on the dark third floor fast. She needed sustenance before Tony arrived, and she sprinted up to the third floor using the hidden stairway from the Abyss. The brief meeting with Anneke was the furthest thing from her mind right now; she needed to prepare. She got out on the floor through the hidden door, and she was in a similar outfit from the first night they had met. Her only change was that her leather pants were skintight to show off her curves and a halter top that barely covered her. She had on the cutest leather motorcycle hat with a chain just above the visor. With her motorcycle jacket she wore the first night, she felt she was a knockout, and it was a good thing she had left them in the Abyss before she left. Within moments, she had four men interested in her, and she swore two women too. She had choice of any she wanted, but she had just enough time for one. So bigger the better in her eyes, and she had just what she wanted right in front of her. Next was to coax him into a less-populated area and then feed upon this fool so she could keep control around Tony. Moments later, she had given a subtle suggestion and used lust and a shake of her hips to move to a very dark corner. After making out for a moment, Michelle's thorn darted so fast out of her mouth and punctured his jugular with pinpoint precision and slipped inside. She began to feed quietly, and this guy had never felt a thing, but he had just quivered. Her mouth was right near his neck, and just then, her fangs latched in, and she closed her eyes. As she expected, he moaned a little since she was doing this lightly, and then her heart reversed. She stopped just as fast and slowly retracted her thorn as the fangs let go of his flesh. She closed the wound with a bit of her blood and a lick from her split tongue and dropped him to the nearby chair and stood up. She then ran her fingers over her lips gently to wipe off leftovers and then licked them clean. She was amazed by how sweet the essence was, but she needed every drop of essence to avoid mistakes tonight. As she walked back toward the hidden door, she reminded herself to fix her jet-black lipstick before she went to meet Tony. She wanted to make sure his mind was blown tonight, and she felt she had fed enough, for now. Now was a time to be patient, Michelle thought to herself; later on, her lover would be a banquet for her to enjoy when she took her third, but right now, her mind was on her first at the moment.

An hour later, the black limousine pulled up, and Tony got out and was met by two people at the club entrance and brought him right in the doors. There on the first floor leaning against the wall, with one foot casually on it, was Michelle waiting for him. She was dressed in a short white halter top that barely covered her, skintight leather pants with slit open sides that were held closed by leather braiding, along with the very same knee-high stiletto boots from the first night they met. The same leather jacket was left casually open to show off her amazing body, and to top it off, she wore a classic leather bikers' hat, and her long shiny black locks of hair ran down the faded jacket just showing her off even more. Her makeup was done perfectly and accented with bright black hues; glossy lips finished the package. Tony was absolutely blown away, and this was his date tonight! She grinned mischievously but never moved, just stared at him seductively.

"He, stranger, you miss me yet?" she asked with a sultry voice, and she was sure he had just melted hearing that.

Tony was so blown away all he could do was stare. She liked this, she really did, because he was quite pleased. She took a few slinky steps toward him like a stripper, and her boots clicked along the marble floors. She then ran her ruby-red nails under his chin trying to get his attention as she circled him like an exotic dancer.

"Oh, come on, sugar, it's just me, little ole me. Looks like the cat's got your tongue though. But this is all yours tonight, so snap out of it, let's have some fun," she said with a grin on her glossy black lips and perfect skin.

Tony felt like he was broken for a moment. Michelle was a full-blown ten tonight! But her nails touching him brought him back.

"My god...you're more beautiful...than the first time I saw you," he said, letting out a long breath to steady himself.

She took his hand, and together they walked into the bar on the first floor. All the while, she thought her first was going to be so easy. Michelle had begun to subtly focus her lust on him, and it would only amplify his own for her. Sooner or later, he would hardly be able to resist her. Michelle was going slowly though, and she had the power to enslave his mind utterly, but that's not what she wanted at the moment. A Succubus could easily use lust to take control of the person she focused it upon as long as they had lust first. Michelle could practically smell it when Tony walked in and saw her leaning on the wall. Lust was a powerful sin, and when it came to a Succubus, they were the masters of it; sooner or later, he would bend to her— they all did.

A little while later on the second floor, Tony had snapped out of it, or so he thought. But Michelle knew who the queen bitch of this place was tonight. Be damned whoever got in her way. They had been dancing up on the second floor, and even the little drops of sweat made Michelle that much sexier in Tony's eyes. After a while, she took his tie he was wearing casually loose and then used it gently to leash him and to lead him off the dance floor. Michelle strutted right past Iris, with Tony following her from behind as she led him past by his tie over her shoulder casually. Then she winked at her and gave her the finger. Michelle just let Iris know who ran this place and could get whatever she wanted. Iris seethed with rage, but she wasn't going to do a thing after last night either. She looked away, and Michelle led Tony to the back tables. There she had drinks brought as she took her long stiletto boots and put them right up on the table and leaned back in her chair, letting her jacket hang open casually and seductively. Tony had no idea what had gotten into her tonight, but he liked it! Michelle was tantalizing, and she had him eating out of her hand. She liked it too because it was no surprise that she was a very dominant woman. Tony had no idea what she had planned next, but Michelle just grinned and took a seductive sip of her drink. She could sense it, the lust, just dripping off him—he was ready.

A little while later, they walked together into an empty fourth floor with just one couch in the center of the room under a single light from above. She then looked back with a devious gleam in her eyes as she locked the door and started up the music system at a lower volume. She then walked him over to the couch and shoved him into it then flung her motorcycle hat right at him, and it landed in his lap. He tried to get up, but she shook her finger to him with a playful evil grin on her perfect black lips. Michelle then let her leather jacket fall to the floor and let lust explode throughout the room with all the presence she had aimed right at him; subtleties were over now! Then she began to dance so erotically that she had his attention immediately. Michelle had just turned the concert hall into an impromptu strip club, and she was the feature—with just one person in the room for a special private dance!

The she began to circle the couch and playfully ran her fingers through his hair. He tried to look back, but she snapped her fingers and pointed to the front of the room and slowly walked back in front of the couch. He watched as she began to turn, and without warning, her halter top hit the floor! Tony's eyes went wide as she began to dance closer and tossed her leg right up onto the couch, and her long stiletto heel was right near his ear. She leaned down, and her lips got so close to his, but then at the last second, she pulled away with a sexy grin. Michelle began to strut around the couch yet again, her boots clicking loudly as she went by. From behind, something dropped onto his head and then fell into his lap; it was her skimpy lacy bra! She walked right past him with her hands covering her exposed breasts. She had her eyes closed and continued to dance on as lust filled every corner of the room now. In response, Tony was stunned; he never expected this! Michelle then threw her hair back and took her hands away and continued to dance on with her arms held high in the air, showing off everything, with her eyes closed, swaying to the music, and letting him watch on totally enamored. Soon she strutted toward the couch again slowly and then took a seat on the far armrest, leaning all the way back, taking her boots off the floor, staring right at him with the most seductive look he had ever seen; she never took her deep-blue eyes off his. She stayed still for a moment with her knee-high boots still in the air seductively and then began to crawl slowly toward him so seductively, her eyes never looking away as she drew closer.

Meanwhile, Tony was in absolute disbelief as she began to straddle him and continue her dance. He put her hands on her hips, but she swatted them away and continued to dance on. Her bare breasts were inches from his face, and suddenly one of her areolas grazed his lips. She then put her hands on his cheeks and kissed him passionately, shaking him back to reality; but like a thunderbolt, she let loose every amount of lust she had left in her body. Tony's mind could only focus on Michelle; everything was hazed right now. He had no other thoughts but the woman in front of him. If she asked anything, he'd do it right now.

She then leaned down to his ear and then whispered, "You're mine, and I'm yours." Then she kissed him passionately, shaking his very foundations as the raw lust in the room took his body fully, sending him into a sexual stupor.

Then as the music ended, Michelle just continued to kiss him; and while his mind was so clouded, her tongue slid down his neck. In a flash, Michelle's thorn slipped inside without him knowing, quickly entering his flesh, and she began to feed. His essence was so sweet with lust because he was totally infatuated with her, but she only wanted to take little. So she stopped as quick as she started but not before she got to feed for just a moment. His head lolled to the side, letting out a long gasp, not only from both being fed upon but from the mental battering his pleasure center just took. Michelle smiled widely and then giggled a little; she got her first and probably fulfilled at least five or six of his private sexual fantasies too.

Later on, and still very much alone on the fourth floor, Michelle had her head in Tony's lap and her boots casually slung over the arm-rest. He was still a little dazed, and again, she really liked it, but she wasn't sure if it was her feeding on him or his mind still recovering from her surprise striptease. The lust was still hanging heavy in the room, and he was still drunk on it in a way. Either way, this man was now wrapped around her little finger; he belonged to her.

"Just wanted to say welcome back, sugar," she said, knocking him out of his stupor suddenly.

He then grinned a little and then let out a small laugh. "I didn't know there was a strip club in here, Michelle," he said back, still clearing his head.

"Oh, there is, but it's only for the biggest VIPs we have, you know, like you," she said back with a sexy giggle of her own.

Michelle then leaned back a little bit and still had yet to put anything back on, and she stretched a bit too, but she could see he was keeping his head from looking down. She then grabbed his chin playfully and moved his head gently to look at her.

"Hello there, you, yoo-hoo, it's perfectly fine, you know, I'm just half naked, you can look," she said with another laugh.

But Tony still couldn't believe what she had done for him tonight; no one had ever treated him so good. "Thank you for the gift for the academy. God knows they need the money. It's why we went to the tournament—to try to drum up business. Your donation is going to help those kids," he said back trying to loosen up, but he was still feeling overwhelmed.

Michelle was flattered, but she was more interested in him and changed the subject fast, just wanting his undivided attention at the moment. "You're quite welcome, but what I want to say is I'm not asking you to go home with me tonight. This was for your pure pleasure, but I'm not going to cheapen it with easy sex afterward. I do want you quite badly right now, if you must know, but if you've taught me one thing, sometimes it's very good to wait. But when we do finally make love. I promise you one thing: you'll never forget me as long as you give in to me," she said back, running her nails down his chest, teasing him.

He nodded back with a grin of his own and finally ran his fingers through her silky hair, and she smiled back. The look in her eyes said she was quite content right now. They chatted the rest of the night on the fourth floor, and as much as Michelle hated to do it, she had to condition him to come back tomorrow night. She needed her second from him, but she also wanted him so badly. Tony had an elder Succubus lusting badly for him. *He should be quite proud of himself,* she thought.

CHAPTER 12

The next evening and early at the club, the sun had just barely set, but Michelle sat there and swirled her Crown Royal and Cola slowly as the ice rattled off the sides of the glass and let out a bored sigh. After last night with Tony, this seemed like such a letdown in her eyes. Sometimes being able to shadow-walk sucked, because she was able to get to the club most times earlier than Elijah, and he had asked her to come in and watch over early operations. By using a few well-known "bridging points" where the shadows remained constant, she was able to get there as the sun set, but it was taxing on her essence too using her abilities during the dusk. Of course, she needed to feed when she got here, but Michelle hated to do early shifts anyway. Turns out the fourth floor had been rented out, and people had been arriving for a little bit now. Michelle had just left that floor due to the constant stream of older yuppies filing in. She was older than all of them and had found a way to move along with the times, but these lost people just festered in their "glory days," and Michelle found it so droll and annoying.

She was on the second floor now, sipping her drink, and had greeted more early regulars than she liked to. Elijah had been very specific about the situation here, and she was not to hide out in the Abyss like the last time. Michelle took another long drink from her glass and let out yet another bored sigh. She hated this—trapped with people she didn't care about; and at the same time, she was waiting for Tony to arrive later tonight. She had set up another car to get him—and not a limo, like he requested, but that was hours away from now. It was supposed to be special tonight, her second in a series of four. She had cleared that part of the night with Elijah, but it cost her the early shift, and sitting at a nightclub with the early boring people sucked. With Elijah, it was always like this: if you wanted something, you had to give something. What good was immortality if she had to do what she was told most nights.

Michelle upended her drink and shoved the glass down the bar; it was her way of asking for a refill. It was then she caught the scent of something familiar in the air. Her senses were so highly tuned, and as she picked up on this scent, her eyes quickly traced the source to the personal aura that accompanied it. Now Michelle was curious who would be at the club this early that she either knew or recognized a particular scent of. Michelle waved off the bartender as she picked up a glass without looking back at him. Then she followed the scent in the air toward the aura she had locked on to. It was faint, and Michelle subtly weaved her way around the room slowly, trying to get a better look at what had her attention at the moment. Her vision shifted, and now she could see the individual energy of each person in the room too and a world of blazed colors. The scent turned out to be coming from a group of girls—but one girl in particular; a blond was the source of the scent and the aura that accompanied it. But the early crowd was a little busy tonight because Michelle couldn't get a good look at the girl she was tracking, but she had her energy signature though. It seemed like the more she followed discreetly, the closer they got to the doorway that led out. It looked like whatever or whoever had gotten her attention was in the midst of leaving, so she doubled back and walked around toward the hidden back door of the second floor discreetly, trying her best to get closer to this oddity in the club.

In the shadows near the hidden door, Michelle knew she had sensed that girl before who had just left the club. But she needed to get closer to be absolutely sure first. So as she left the club with her friends, Michelle slipped out the hidden door of the room and walked into a long black shadow looming near the hidden stairs. In mere seconds, she emerged from another ink-black shadow in the alley between the Factory and the adjacent building. From there she hugged the wall stealthily and took a quick look down the avenue and spotted what she was looking for. It was her and her friends, but her back was still to her, and Michelle couldn't see her face. Part of her just wanted to storm down there and act as if she had skipped out on a tab. But there were too many people both in front of the club and, combined with her group of friends, would create a scene. Elijah hated that, as much as he hated Michelle damaging the club, so that course of action was definitely out tonight with her plans later. Michelle then watched as people walked down the avenue, and she smirked because she had an idea. Thinking hard, she remembered a few of the patrons from last night and then placed her hands over her face as she stepped back into the shadows of the alley. When she emerged, her entire body, clothes, and face were changed. She looked like just one of the many people she had interacted with at the Factory last night. With her illusion set, she stepped around the corner as if she was walking to the front doors of the club. The girl was still chatting it up with her friends, but they were slowly getting into a cab, so Michelle hurried her pace to get closer quicker. Just as she reached the cab, the last girl stepped into it and shut the door, and the car began to pull away. Michelle took a quick step, almost too quick; thankfully no one noticed but only glanced in the window and saw very little. All she could do was get the cab number and the license plate.

Still on the street out in front of the club, Michelle shook her head and tried not to throw a cursing tirade right there. Tony was going to be here soon, and she needed her second feeding from him before the stroke of midnight. But this girl—she swore she knew her, and now it bothered her too. Walking back toward the alley and into the darkness once again, she took her phone out of her pocket of her jacket. As she turned the corner, she let the illusion go and strode into the same big shadow she had just emerged from before. She was then transported behind the bar of the Abyss and walked toward the hidden elevator door that led to Elijah's offices. Once inside and the doors closed, she made her call. As she expected, it went to voice mail, but it mattered little to her the number was to a pager.

"Hey, sugar, it's you-know-who here. Listen, I've run into a little snag at the club, you know, work shit. I need another hour tonight before you drop by, and I'm so sorry, I'll call the car service. I promise to so make it up to you though, and you're on the list, so just walk right in. I'll meet you at the bar on the ground floor, okay? Ciao," she said and then kissed the air, closing her phone with a resounding snap, and walked out of the elevator at the very top hidden floor of the Factory.

She strode into Elijah's office and was happy that he wasn't there because she was about to be very bad. Then she walked around his broad desk and flopped into his worn leather office chair. She leaned back and put her feet on the desk and, with a quick move of her boots, kicked the phone on the desk to her. She caught the cordless phone and leaned back as she began to dial a number she never thought she'd ever need before. It rung just for a moment, and then someone picked up; and before they could answer, she cut them right off.

"Yes, hello, this is Police Plaza, correct?" Michelle nodded once and sat back as the office chair creaked a little. "This is the Factory over in Chelsea. I need to get the number of a cab company that just had a pickup here," she said and paused for a moment with a grin on her lips. "Why? Well, the driver had come in looking for his fare that he was called for but dropped his wallet. An associate of mine picked it up and rushed outside but missed the cab. We just want to return it, so we need the company name of the dispatcher. I've got the plate and cab ID number too, so they can pick it up," she said, grinning and trying not to giggle at the moment.

Michelle grinned and nodded as she told them the cab's plate number and ID. In moments, she had the dispatcher and hung up with the police; she then began to dial again. She waited as the phone rang, and she began to tap her one foot on her other and watched as her fine leather boots swayed. Finally, someone answered her call, and once again, she cut them off from their greeting.

"Hello, this is the Factory over in Chelsea, and we just had someone use one of your cabs to leave the club, and they never paid their tab. So, before we call the police and give them the cab's info, we'd like to see if they'd rather settle up first. I've got the cab number and plate, could you tell me who called it in and where it dropped off the fare from the Factory a few moments ago?" she said to them grinning and then kicked a pad to the edge of the desk and then grabbed it.

There was always a pen on the pad, and Michelle caught the gold pen before it fell to the floor. She listened for a moment and then nodded again. "No, I don't recognize the name, but you're sure of the drop-off, correct? Yes, I've got an idea where that is. We can take care of this. No need to get the police involved, and no, the driver isn't in trouble with us in the least bit. I doubt he was involved at all. Stuyvesant, correct, we'll send one of our security staff down there with the tab and hope they can catch them, and I hope it was just a misunderstanding. We'd rather keep the police out of it if we can. It helps the club's image though," she said fast and then began to get annoyed with the person on the phone now.

Michelle listened to whomever was on the phone prattle on for a moment, then she unceremoniously hung up. She had the cab's destination, but the name, she really didn't know, and then she stood up walking toward yet another shadow in the office, only to vanish yet again in the darkness.

A little while later, she was in Stuyvesant, and this was never a place Michelle liked at the early part of the night, but she had caught up with the cabbie who had said he dropped the fare off at a local coffeehouse. Then a barista at the establishment had told her she overheard that the girls had left on foot heading to a small eatery heading toward the East Village. Michelle followed on foot and then touched one of the many lampposts on the street and closed her eyes briefly. She felt her environment and searched for the specific energy who had passed by recently, trying to locate that girl's aura and energy signature again. Her quarry had gone to the left, and she headed that way as she watched as the leftover auras hung now like a path for her to follow. From there she hurried across the street, and she was getting annoyed too. She was getting farther away from her car, and this was starting to get to be too long of a search for her, and Michelle then glanced down at her watch. Her beautiful Cartier watch that said she now had just under forty-five minutes before Tony arrived at the club. Part of her just wanted to go back to her car, but her curiosity was aroused about this mystery girl she had met somewhere before; the scent was pretty unique and getting stronger as she followed.

The trail led her to a small restaurant, and before Michelle went inside, she used an illusion to cover her face. Once inside, she was seated near a window right behind where the girls from the club had congregated. She began to think that being an empath had its advantages some nights, but others not so much. After sitting there for fifteen minutes listening to them laugh and chat, the smell that had caught her attention in the first place was heavy in the air now, but she was getting annoyed. She sipped her cup of coffee and thought it was horrible but watched the blonde intently. Her back was still to her, and she was still unable to see her face again, and this was starting to get on her nerves. It seemed like the girls were getting ready to leave again, and they were all heading home from here. Michelle wasn't about to follow again, she had big plans, but she just had to know who this was now. Just then the blonde began to get up and turned slowly toward Michelle, and she finally saw her face clearly. Seeing who it was, she nearly spit out her horrible coffee right on to the booth table she was sitting at! It was Tony's ex-girlfriend Ashley, and she had only seen her from the pictures in Tony's room and locker when she had been looking for him a few nights ago. Her scent lingered in his bedroom because of the time they had spent together so long ago. Michelle then frowned and began to seethe with anger. What was she doing in her club? Looking for her Tony? Someone must have told her he had been hanging out there and about Michelle, since they had been spending a lot of time together. Tony had gone there with friends before, and one of them must have told her. Michelle then watched as a few of the girls walked past her, and Ashley headed to the restrooms first. She then waited a moment, dropped twenty dollars on the table, and then got up. This bitch was getting set straight right here and right now. In her eyes, Tony belonged to her now; and if there was one thing Michelle Victoria Du'Pree wasn't in the mood for, it was competition for her man's affections. It was time for this girl to realize the old adage—finders keeper, losers weepers. Michelle got to the door, looked over her shoulder once more, and made sure no one was heading in too. With that she walked inside the restaurant restroom behind Ashely.

Inside the old restroom, Michelle turned on the water at one of the three sinks there and then gazed into the mirror on the wall. Her face came into view as the illusion faded away, and she shook out her hair. She waited till the stall door opened and Ashley began to wash her hands, and Michelle shut the water in the sink she had been running. She turned toward her and was trying not to let her anger get the better of her right now.

"Ashley, right?" she said to her, and then she glanced over at her.

Her hazel-brown eyes and shoulder-length blond hair looked just like the photo in Tony's room. She was taller than Michelle, but that mattered little in her eyes. She was a pretty young girl, with a well-built figure and very attractive face. But she seemed a little confused and also worried that a total stranger knew her name, but she tried her best not to be overly concerned either.

"Yes, do I know you because I can't place your face right now," she said back to her with a smooth voice and a warm smile.

Michelle began to walk toward the door and stopped, blocking the way out. "Oh, you don't know me, but I sure know you. So, I'm going to be as cordial as I can here since I was raised to be a lady in public. Tony isn't yours anymore. I know all about your time off from each other," she said with a sarcastic look in her eyes. "This is the only time I'm being nice about this, but in simple terms, go and find someone else because he's taken now," Michelle finished with an evil grin on her full red lips.

Ashley just glared back at her in disbelief. All because of this girl she didn't even know, talking to her like that, her eyes narrowed at Michelle. "Bitch, I don't know who you think you are or what your problem is, but Tony's a big boy, and he can make his own decisions too. It's true we took time off, but I've realized my mistake, and we've got history too. So next time, just fuck off, let him decide," she said back, taking a step toward Michelle with an annoyed scowl on her face, but Michelle stared her down defiantly.

"Since we've thrown manners out the window here, I'll make it simpler for you. Yes, I'm a bitch, and yes, you have history with him too, but guess what, you're history now too, ancient history. You left, and I stepped in, and now it's time for you take off again. Don't come to the club and think you're taking what's mine now. I'm the wrong person to even consider trying that with—trust me. Oh, and it's Ms. Bitch to you," she said back with an angry glare in her eyes and a smug grin on her lips.

Ashley began to walk toward the door again and stared back angrily at Michelle as she did. "So, you're the little club whore who he's been spending time with. Honey, you're a fling, get it through your inflated head. I've heard all about you, and you've got money, and you think who the fuck you are, but when I get to talk to Tony next, guess whose gonna be history, you!" she said back gruffly and stormed past Michelle and walked out the restroom door.

Michelle's eyes looked toward the floor, and then she shook her head; she just had to disrespect her like that. Ashley's aura trail was easy enough to see, and she had her scent now too. Tracking her would be simple, but what was hers, was hers in her eyes. Michelle looked up and then, with a single swipe of her hand, shattered one of the bulbs from the three overhead lights that lit the room. This created even more shadows, and Michelle walked into one and vanished but was completely infuriated at the moment.

A short time later, Ashley was walking down the street and toward the nearest subway station to take her back to Queens, and she was so angry at the moment. She planned on talking to Tony first thing in the morning about whoever that was at the restaurant. She walked down the station stairs and made a left turn. But all of a sudden, something or someone grabbed her, and everything went black, then surreal cold surrounded her body. Minutes seemed like hours, and she was dumped onto her side roughly, overlooking Chelsea Piers again. Her body was numb and shivering along with her vision blurred but slowly coming back, then her hearing began to clear. Last thing that came back to her was her sense of smell, and she caught the scent of the pier at night and the subtle scent of roses and jasmine on the breeze. She slowly looked over her shoulder, still freezing and shivering, and saw someone leaning up against the wall away from the pier waiting for her to come around.

Then she heard the sound of boots clicking along, walking the ground slowly, as the distorted figure came into view finally, but it was her voice that gave her away. "I told you I was a bitch, and you should've walked away. Go find someone else, it's a big world, someone's out there or was out there for you," the familiar voice said to her as the blurry figure drew closer to her.

Ashely knew this voice from before, at the restaurant, and focused her eyes. "You...it's you...what did you do to me...?" she said through trembling blue lips.

Michelle walked past her and then began to circle like a predator. "My name is Michelle Victoria Du'Pree, and I bet you've heard of me if you've been to *my* club. You see I warned you to back off, go away, but you had to threaten, and you thought I was nothing. You thought wrong, bitch, and that's going to cost you," she said in a mocking voice that was doing its best to hide the anger and rage behind it.

Still sprawled on the dirty pier, Ashley was shivering uncontrollably, but whatever she was saying made no sense. She had no idea Tony was involved with the club owner, let alone a Du'Pree; they were royalty in the city's upper society, but still she wasn't backing down either. "You did this to me...whatever it was, it's assault... you're not getting away with it...I promise," she said back, and her voice still trembled because she was colder than she had ever been in her entire life.

Michelle stopped circling and knelt down in front of her. She then grabbed her chin to gaze at her right in the eyes, and her deep blue orbs seemed to burn with an unnatural fire behind them. "You're not in the position to either threaten or promise anything right now," she said back, letting go of her chin roughly. "You're going to threaten me now. Look at yourself on the ground, and yes, I did that to you too. But I doubt highly you're going to say anything," Michelle said back, standing up again.

Ashley tried to stand but couldn't because she was so cold. Just then Michelle moved so fast like a blur and roughly grabbed her, pulling her to her feet. Then she was lifted off her feet and slammed her into a wall by her throat! *How can a petite girl possess strength like this?* was all Ashley could think at the moment as her body shivered yet again.

The pain of hitting the wall was bad enough, but then one of her shoulders burned, and warm fluid ran down her skin. She looked over at her shoulder and gasped because a monstrous claw had dug into her flesh, and a horrible feeling pulsed through her body. She looked down to see Michelle holding her against the wall, her eyes burning with such hatred.

"What's mine stays mine, bitch! You should have listened, but you thought yourself better than me too. I was a little club whore, as you said, not worth your attention, you say, a fling, a nobody. Honey, you picked the wrong bitch to piss off tonight!" she growled back at her, spearing her flesh further with a painful twist of her clawed hand. Pinned to the wall and in Michelle's grasp, Ashley tried to scream out but couldn't; the pain and the numbness she was in was too much. "What did I do to you before you asked me? I dragged you through the shadows, its why you're so cold. You don't belong there, just like you don't belong in his life anymore either. As for what's happening to you, the poison from my claw has paralyzed you too. You're going to die tonight, little Ashley. No human has talked that way to me in over three decades. Who the fuck do you think you are?" Michelle said, enraged, twisting her long talonlike claw, pulling it free.

Then she let Ashley drop to the ground, and she slid down the wall and into a sitting position. Michelle then walked past and grabbed Ashley's hair, dragging her on the ground closer to the pier. With a simple gesture of her hand, she tossed her like a rag doll toward the edge of the pier, still very much paralyzed. With a snap of her wrist, the long black claws shed the blood that was coating them to the ground. The last bit of blood left, Michelle licked off her pinky talon with a low growl escaping her beautiful lips.

"All you had to do was go away. You left him, he didn't leave you. He was miserable when I met him, but now, he's happy, because of *me!*" Michelle said, slowly walking toward her again. "I gave you the opportunity to do just that again, walk away, but now we've come too far. You pissed me off, and for most people, it's the last thing you do. Most times I try my best to keep my composure, but tonight, I just don't see that happening," she said, stalking ever closer, and a louder animalistic growl once more menaced her.

Ashley looked up at Michelle when she was almost on top of her again. "What…in God's name…are…you?" she said through a weak voice, and a dry short gasp escaped her lips then.

"More than you'll ever understand in the small moments you have left," Michelle said back coldly, and with that, her head leaned back slightly, and her lower jaw began to tremble roughly.

In horror, Ashley watched as Michelle's lower jaw seemed like it dislocated with a sick snap, and her mouth fell open loosely. Then her tongue emerged from her mouth slowly and lengthened, finally splitting, with Michelle's sharp thorn emerging from the flesh; and from the end of each of the split tongue, two smaller fangs slid free and snapped angrily. Ashley wanted to scream, but she was frozen in fear. She had never seen something so beautiful become so hideous so fast! Michelle drew closer, and Ashley tried to fight, to get up and run. But Michelle snatched her up like a toy again and ran the sharp appendage from her mouth down her throat, as if she was savoring something. Ashley tried to hit her, but it did little, and Michelle's sharp thorn scratched its way down her neck, drawing blood, and slowly it pierced her chest, opening up her aorta by digging in under her flesh, and then it vanished. Ashley whimpered in pain, and tears streamed down her cheeks as the sharp thorn dug in so deeply, but then the smaller fangs snapped closed, and the barbs embedded into her flesh, delivering a numbing anesthetic. Michelle then roughly thrusted her thorn in deeper and began to feed from Ashley as it pierced her heart. In turn, Michelle's own heart shifted, and the suction became so strong. Ashley pounded with everything she had left, but she was just too powerful. She grabbed at her tongue still in her flesh to try to pull it free, but it was too slippery! Michelle in turn grabbed her hand and snapped it like a dry twig, and Ashley tried to cry out again, but she punched her hard in the ribs. The essence was sour-sweet, with the full tang of fear as Michelle drank greedily. Blackness closed in as Ashley began to fade away. She felt like something was tearing at her very soul, and she knew she was dying. But Michelle never stopped and lost herself to the feeding, and just then, she felt Ashley's soul rip loose; and just like that, she consumed it! Her last memories flooded into Michelle's mind, and her thorn ripped free with a sickly sucking noise. Coagulated blood oozed from the wound now that her body was devoid of essence because Michelle had consumed every drop rapidly.

She looked down at Ashley's dead body, her stark-white eyes staring back at her, and angrily she hurled the body into the river with ease. Michelle then walked back toward the shadows and vanished. Only to appear moments later on the rooftop of the Factory. She had Ashley's last thoughts still fresh in her mind. She shook her head and tried to let go of the thoughts, but it was hard even for her.

"I'm not a fucking monster, you bitch!" she screamed out loud, and then her fist battered the wall, cracking the concrete. "I'm only protecting what's mine! You'll see, he cares about me, now and soon forever!" Michelle hissed and then began to walk toward the rooftop doors to meet with Tony.

As she headed inside, she stopped at a mirror in the hallway to look herself over. The essence she had absorbed from her moment consuming Ashley's soul had made her look radiant. It would be tough for Tony not to be smitten with her tonight again. Best yet, after feeding so well, it would make it much easier for her to control herself while she took her second from him. As she strode toward the elevator, she thought to herself, *Thank you, Ashley. I'll put what you've given me to good use.* She then let out a small snicker as the doors to the elevator closed.

CHAPTER 13

A little while later, Tony arrived at the Factory in a pretty average town car—until you got inside, that is. This car had every amenity you'd ever want if you're traveling in luxury but incognito. He began to get out, but Michelle met him at the curbside and just got in with him. After last night, he couldn't believe she was stunning yet again. She wasted no time and kissed him as she used her other hand to slam the door shut behind her. Damn it, she wanted to take him home and have him there and then her second too. Strangely enough, she was highly aroused after feasting tonight. But she decided not to, and as the driver got in, she stopped kissing him. She was content right now after eliminating the competition and having him utterly to herself; she could wait for that perfect moment to make love for their first time. The driver asked her where to take them, and Michelle wanted to go to Central Park tonight. She had an idea before, and she felt that he should at least have a chance to know what she truly was. Tonight, she was going to give him that chance; if he figured out something was wrong, then she'd tell him right away. If not, then fate was on her side, and she would tell him after the fact.

When they arrived at the park, Michelle took Tony by the hand and walked with him through the cool night air, hardly caring because she really didn't. They made their way to the pavilion where the horse-drawn carriages were, and the horses began to get spooked at her approach. It was because they could sense what she was, but Tony couldn't understand it at all. The closer she got, the more spooked they were. Tony inquired about a carriage ride but was told to come back in an hour. So he and Michelle decided to take a walk through the park, and she halfway hoped to get mugged tonight. She loved the park at night; most times the chances of finding a perfect meal here was easy enough for a pretty Succubus. That would be fate if one presented itself tonight, and when she finished with them, she would have to come clean to Tony too. She walked with him without a care in the world but kept her eye on her watch. She had to mind the time, but it was early enough yet; time for a bit of fun, she thought.

A little while later, Michelle was very disappointed in the city's criminals and thugs tonight. She guessed it was the autumn chill in the air or just blind dumb luck, but nothing happened. When they left the park, they decided to leave Fifth Avenue and head for Park Drive. Michelle had always wanted to live around here again, so this felt like it was the perfect time to browse places for them very soon. As she walked along, she kept trying to do very subtle things to get his attention. Mostly causing illusions and then making them vanish. She scared the hell out of a few pedestrians, which she thought was hilarious, but Tony never noticed, she guessed—weird, and through the city they went hand in hand. He just walked along with her giving her his undivided attention. Could this be fate, she wondered, but one of the biggest attempts was when Tony bought them both hot coffee from a little shop. He told her it was very hot, but Michelle took a long drink from her cup without worry. Immortals were very resistant to heat, she guessed, from their demonic nature, and this cup wasn't as hot for her. He noticed it but just asked if she was okay, and Michelle didn't lie; she said she was fine. She was starting to really think that she was destined to take Tony and explain later.

As they made their way back to Central Park for their carriage ride, Michelle and Tony decided to take a shortcut through the park. When they made a quick turn down a darkened path, Tony noticed that the lamp had been broken on purpose. He seemed a bit on edge, but Michelle, on the other hand, grinned widely. All she could think was that maybe the city wasn't going to disappoint her tonight when it came to the hazards of Central Park at night. Together they walked hand in hand past the broken glass, and that's when someone stepped out in front of them from the side of the path. He was a big man, and when Tony said, "Excuse me," he stepped in front of him again. From behind them, another man stepped out, keeping them from walking back the way they had come. He just stood there, and Tony looked back fast and had Michelle get behind him as he turned away from the two of them now. From the opposite side of the same path, another man stepped out, and then there was the loud click of a switchblade. Tony looked over right away and continued to hold Michelle's hand and keep her away from the three of them now. Michelle had never had someone just put himself in harm's way for her, and all she wanted to do was attack the three of them now. The man with the knife walked closer, and the one from behind them before closed in too. Tony just shook his head and still kept himself between them and Michelle now; they weren't going to get near her without a fight.

"Look, guys, I've only got a few bucks in my wallet and maybe a few subway tokens and train ticket too. I think you picked the wrong people to mug, but if you want them, then I'll give them up. Just don't hurt the lady, okay?" Tony said to them, and the one holding the knife laughed a little.

"Hey, asshole, you don't think we can see that jewelry she's wearing tonight, those nice earrings, the necklace, and her rings too? I bet she's got some money as well in that expensive Gucci purse on her shoulder. She looks like a Park Avenue rich bitch to me. So how about we skip your wallet and see what the girl's got? Tell her to take off the jewelry first then hand over her purse, maybe even that nice jacket she's wearing too, hmmm?" the thug with the knife said, getting closer, and Tony shook his head.

"I told you, you can have my wallet and such, but her, you leave alone," Tony said back to them, and the one in front of them reached for Michelle hearing that.

Michelle grinned with anticipation seeing how this was playing itself out. The moment he grabbed her, she would turn on him fast and then deal with the other two. It looked like she was going to have some explaining to do afterward. Tony was going to know what she was, and hopefully he would accept her and then her gift too. The large man went to grab her, and faster than most humans, Tony's hands snapped forward and stopped him. He blocked the man's initial grab, and then when he tried to punch Tony, he blocked that too. In moments, Michelle was in awe. Tony's hands moved like a blur, and he quickly struck a man with a combination of punches that easily outweighed him by more than thirty pounds. The strikes staggered him easily, and when he threw another punch at Tony, he caught it and then used his momentum to land a huge strike to his head, knocking him to the ground, groaning from the series of blows. Blood ran from the man's nose and lip, but he never budged when he fell to his back.

"GET THAT MOTHERFUCKER," the knife-wielding thug screamed out, and the other man rushed at Tony, throwing a very lazy punch, and Tony pushed Michelle away from the fight again.

Easily Tony intercepted the punch and struck him once to the throat and then to the head and lastly flipped him over onto his back and finished with a strike to his face faster than Michelle had ever seen a human move! The last man swung the knife once and then again, and Tony jumped out of the way both times. The last time he tried to strike with the knife, Tony grabbed his arm and bent it at an awkward angle fast. The knife fell from his hand, and Tony kicked it into the bushes. He then flipped the man over, and he landed face-down on the pavement with a loud slam. Michelle then watched as Tony torqued his arm roughly when he tried to get up again. And applied a choke hold to his throat from behind. She watched as the thug finally gave up and began to turn blue, but Tony never let him go as she drew closer.

"Now, you stay down here, and the lady and I will be on our way. If I see you even try to get up, you'll wake up in the hospital next. Now we're going to be on our way. You count to fifty, and then you can get up and help your friends out of the park. Next time, take the easy cash and don't try to exploit women, it makes me mad. By the way, you better get the two of them to the hospital also," Tony said to him and torqued his arm one more time and then let go and stood up.

He had Michelle walk a little farther down the path, and then he followed her, never turning his back on the three thugs. Once they were far enough away, he took her hand and began to walk toward the horse paddocks again. When they were back in the light, he turned toward her and tried to smile like nothing had happened.

"You okay? You looked a little shocked in there before," Tony asked her as they got closer to the horse paddocks and to more people.

"No one ever did anything like that for me. Most times I would have to deal with that myself," she said back with a smile and squeezed his hand.

Tony said nothing back as they got closer to the carriages, and he quickly waved off the incident. Michelle, on the other hand, just realized that Tony was to be hers—she believed it now. She was prepared to kill the three of them for that, but he stepped in and defended her without a thought. There was no doubt in her mind now Tony would accept his new life with her; there was no need to utter a word and risk his life any further. This was to be her prodigy; she believed it now.

They arrived back at the paddocks for the carriage ride, and for some unknown reason, the horses never got upset around Michelle this time. She walked right past them, and not one of them were spooked. To her, this was the sign she was looking for; she would tell Tony all about her after he was Immortal too. Now her thoughts revolved around her second feeding and when would be the opportune time to do just that. Michelle then grinned to herself and began to weave lust around her. Slowly she began to draw Tony in like she had before. Sooner or later, he would be wrapped around her little finger again. He was very susceptible to her charms now, and Tony had been exposed to them quite a few times. Soon the driver called to them to climb aboard the carriage, and Michelle began to look for the opportunity she was looking for. She was holding his hand; her lustful charms were faced right at Tony, and all she could think was add in some romance, and soon she would be utterly irresistible to him.

IN THE NAME OF SIN

The brisk night in Central Park made for a great tour ride around it. Michelle sat back in the old carriage remembering when there were thousands of these here. Life was much simpler back then, and her mind wandered a bit while Tony held her tightly to keep her warm. When he began to kiss her, this was the perfect chance to attempt her second. Michelle created an illusion that enveloped both her and Tony. To anyone who saw, it was two young lovers sharing a long passionate kiss. Then she amplified her presence, enthralling him like she had last night, and lust filled him easily. From there she took a moment to find a perfect spot and placed Tony's hand on her breast to distract him. As they finished their second kiss, Michelle went for a third but started to kiss his neck softly. She felt the carotid artery pulse lightly, and with a quick gesture of her tongue, her sharp thorn slipped into his neck painlessly with a slight lick. She tasted his essence once more—so sweet with lust, and she began to feed softly at first, and she held him tightly. This time she drank deeply, unlike last night, and he moaned a little in delight and pulled her close to him, and his essence was so rich. Michelle took his hand, flooding him with her pleasures she was experiencing, and he relaxed in her arms. Barely a minute or two passed, and Michelle closed the wound easily. She had her second, but Tony wasn't feeling well afterward. She hadn't expected him to embrace her like that during her feeding, and she lost herself in the moment; he had interfered, and it almost created a disaster. When Immortals fed, it was very hard to control the moment; that subtle embrace had been enough to disturb her concentration. She could only hope the carriage ride would give him time to rest. He needed it because he had just been fed deeply upon by an elder by complete accident. Michelle looked at her watch and noticed the time. That was close; she had four minutes left before the stroke of midnight. She had to be more careful next time.

When the carriage ride was over, Michelle watched Tony climb down and try to keep his shaky legs under him. If he wasn't an athlete, he would've fallen trying to get out of the carriage. She rushed over to him and helped him stay on his feet. He kept saying that the adrenaline from the fight before had worn off and it had to be his nerves. The driver asked what was wrong, but Michelle lied by saying

109

he had some hot coffee from before, but it was disagreeing with him. She paid the driver and tipped him double for his troubles. Her heart was breaking right now seeing Tony trying to recover on a cold park bench, sitting there completely dazed. She had seen this before in the club, but never up close like this. She had taken too much, but he had been so sweet to her, and his essence was so arousing, then he unexpectedly embraced her, but she should've stopped earlier. Michelle called her driver, and he helped Tony to the car slowly. She could've lifted him, but that was taking the game from before a bit too far. As he got in the car, Michelle had the driver stop so she could get him some water and a small cup of tea that he could sip. He had to start feeling better; she was going to be so upset about this because she had her second but needed her third tonight. She had the driver begin the long drive to Queens and told him to drive slowly so he didn't get sick. Now he thought he had come down with something suddenly, but Michelle could only soothe him in the back seat the best she could.

After a little while, the color began to come back to his face slowly, and he started to snap out of his daze. Michelle began to feel a little bit better, but as they got closer to his home, she hated what was coming next though. She had to condition him again to return tonight to the club, and she hated that now. She wanted to let him rest due to the mistake, but she had no choice; if he didn't come back, she would have to start over. Once they pulled up, Michelle watched him get out of the car and had the driver stay parked until he was safely inside. All she could think was telling him, *Go sleep it off, and come back to me tomorrow, once more.* Michelle then realized that for him to survive this, she had to be much more dominating and not allow another unexpected mistake like that again. If that had happened during her fourth, they would both be dead. She then instructed the driver to take her back to the Factory.

CHAPTER 14

Later that afternoon in Queens, Tony rolled out of bed, and his neck hurt along with still feeling a bit ill. He couldn't understand what happened; the fight was one thing, but on the carriage ride, he never got the chance to tell Michelle that he loved her. It was supposed to be a moment that he hoped would change things for both of them in their brief relationship. He half walked, half stumbled into the kitchen and noticed that he was home alone again. His sister was at school, and his mom was working one of her many jobs. He saw her so little these days, but she'd left a few college brochures for him to go through so he could start studying to become a physical therapist like he wanted. There was a note was from his mother as well, to get to work on these applications very soon please. His mom had worked night and day since his dad had left to send both him and his sister, Marissa, to college. She was still two and a half years away from graduation, but Tony had graduated almost a year and a half ago. Most of his friends from high school had moved on to college by now, and he felt he was the only one just wasting his time in Queens. He sat down and tried to read the brochures and fill out applications, but his head was pounding. The cold coffee from yesterday wasn't helping either. He felt like hell, but he had promised Michelle he would come and see her again, and he didn't want to disappoint her. Again, he started to think if they did become serious, how would he introduce Michelle to his family? He had no idea about anything going on in life lately, and it felt like it was spiraling out of control. He had tried out for the Olympic Martial Arts Team last year when it was available, but he missed the regular team by two points and was asked to be an alternate. That meant in the event something happened, he could get asked to fill in. Then he got hurt and got removed from the alternate team, so that was over. Worse yet, he had to watch the games now instead of living them—not what he had been hoping for, so he had started to get serious about going to school, but even that seemed like a long shot these days too. He thought maybe getting something to eat would make him feel better, but the sight of food nauseated him. What was wrong with him? And he was thinking, should he go and see Michelle tonight being sick like this? Still, she was so looking forward to this, and she was all he had at the moment going right in his life. He had to go tonight. Maybe a few more hours of sleep would help. With that he went back to his room and crawled into his bed again. Still, he couldn't figure out why he wanted to sleep so badly right now; soon his eyes shut, and he fell into a deep sleep again.

*****

A few hours later in SoHo, Michelle had just woken up and had her flat cleaned last night while she was out. It was spotless, and she had chosen this as where she would attempt to give Tony her dark gift. But first she needed to get past tonight's third time feeding on him. She felt horrible about how things had worked out last night and hoped so much he had recovered. Still, she had to try one more time with him, and then she could give him three days to rest before her final attempt at creation. She slowly got dressed, and she had called the car service last night to go and get him. He should be picked up soon, and tonight was so special. Her third would mark him if done correctly, and if it cast the reddish aura upon his body, that was the sign that he was ready to brave death; he was her chosen. But she had to be careful when her lust inversed it would make it very difficult to resist him. But she had felt this before and felt her age and discipline would be able to handle it though. She then had three nights to attempt creating him, and she had chosen the third and final night. Rebirth was never easy, and the risks were massive, but she had to try. Michelle finished getting dressed, and once again, she looked amazing. She then walked out the front doors of her flat and took her phone out of her purse as she got into the limo. One more call, and the night was all set; Tony would rest well after this—if he survived, that is, which she hoped with all her heart he did.

Later at the Factory, a polished town car pulled up with Tony in it, and he was hoping Michelle had a nice quiet night planned for them. He was feeling a little better when he woke up early in the evening, but his neck was still a bit sore. He was still trying to figure out how he could've hurt it in that scuffle in the park. Tony began to get out, and just like last night, Michelle came rushing down the stairs and hopped into the car with him. She kissed him immediately and closed the door with her foot this time.

"Tell me you're you feeling better?" she asked with a worried look on her face.

"I'm better. I just can't figure out what happened to me last night, is all," he said back, still looking a bit confused but more embarrassed than anything else.

She then playfully put her hands over his ears and said something to the driver. Michelle looked excited tonight, and that meant she was up to something. The car left and drove them to Midtown, closer to Times Square. Michelle just cuddled next to Tony, and everything seemed so right. She knew what she was doing felt like the right decision, and she slowly began to weave lust around him and herself. Soon the car pulled up to a huge luxury hotel, and Michelle got out and took Tony with her inside. Then she told him to wait in the lobby and then had a small conversation with the front desk. Next, she walked over and led him to the grand ballroom that was unoccupied at this time. She took off her jacket and asked Tony to take off his too. She then took his hand and led him out to the dark dance floor as her presence began to intensify. Then she took his other hand and smiled widely, placing it on her body.

"Dance with me," she asked him with her arms held out wide.

"There's no music, Michelle," he answered, drawing closer to her.

She looked up at him. "We are the music, silly. Dance with me," she said, pointing to his heart.

Together they swayed slowly, and Michelle put her head on his chest and felt him holding her so tightly. She had been right to select him; she felt she belonged with him. Together they danced to nothing more but the rhythm of their heartbeats. She listened on, and it was the sweetest music she had ever heard in her life. Moments later, Tony did what she never expected tonight. He broke the silence and then said something she couldn't believe. Michelle stopped dancing and looked up at him still a little confused.

"Say that again please, I didn't hear you clearly," she said back, needing to hear it again.

Tony let go of her and then took a step back. "Don't make me say it again, it was hard enough to say the first time," he said back, but she took a step toward him, but he stepped away too.

"No, please just say it again," she said back, a little louder this time.

Tony swallowed hard and then spoke again, "Michelle Du'Pree, I love you," he said softly.

She closed her eyes and felt her right hand ball into a fist. She had to ask herself once again, why? She tried to think straight, but deep down, she realized in her heart of hearts that she loved him too. Her hand relaxed, and she took another step toward him, but he stepped away again. Then she saw it: his aura, love, and just hope with a little bit of fear mixed in. She felt it radiating from him; he just wanted her, nothing else. He wasn't looking for anything else, just her love; and Michelle's steeled heart, the one she guarded for so long, melted in just a second, and love filled her body for the first time in so long. She immediately stopped weaving lust around the room and took a step toward him.

"Don't you want my answer?" she said back, smiling in a way Tony had never seen before.

He stopped stepping away, and Michelle closed the gap between them. She put her arms around him, and then her strange grin turned into a wide smile. "Antonio Willhiem, I've known for so long that I loved you but denied it. You're what makes my life worth living these days and nights. So yes, I love you too," she said, closing her eyes with such love in her heart and placing her head on his chest again.

Tonight, she hated being an Immortal, because if she could've, she would've cried tears of sheer joy. She held him tighter, and he would be hers forever; she wanted no other. Once their dance was over, she had him gather their jackets, and she practically ran to the front desk again. They met just outside the ballroom and ran down the hallway together laughing. She hit the button on the elevator, and as soon as the doors opened, and a few people got out, she walked in with him and shut the door. When the door shut, Michelle leaped into his arms, and her lips met his; her skin set ablaze for the first time. She felt love, real love, and it felt wonderful to her; it had been so long! Together they crashed into the walls, and Tony held her tightly in his arms as her legs wrapped around his waist. The elevator went all the way to the top floor, and as the doors opened, Michelle and Tony almost fell out of the doors together. They were still kissing when they entered the hallway, hardly looking where they were going. She pointed to the left, and he scooped her up and carried her, walking down the hallway to the door at the end. Michelle took out the key and awkwardly opened the lock, and together they stepped into the room, and with a swift kick of her boot, the door closed once he carried her inside.

Hours later

If Tony thought Michelle was overly dominant during the striptease two nights ago, he had just been reintroduced to that side while they made love. She was on top of him, and she had pinned his arms down and wouldn't let him go. Every time he tried to move, she stopped him yet again. She was so enthralling, but she wouldn't let him join in with her yet. Foreplay had taken so long, but now she was in charge. She then leaned down and kissed him in a teasing manner, pushing his hands away again.

"Submit to me, Tony, give in, let go, and trust in me. You'll never forget me if you do," Michelle whispered into his ear and then drew his earlobe into her mouth with her lips, making him shiver.

Tony let go and let her have her way and relaxed. He stopped fighting her, and she sped up riding him quickly and put her hands on his chest, releasing his hands, but he didn't move, and she was right! She flooded him with her pleasures and let out a seductive moan of pure pleasure. Michelle was amazing, and she had him wrapped around her heart! Moments later, they both climaxed, with her grabbing Tony's hands and placing them on her body, allowing him to join in finally. He grabbed her hair and rolled her to the side and then to her back, and she didn't fight like before; she let out a contented sigh. Her legs wrapped around his back as they continued on. She was about to cry out again, but her hands ran down his back, leaving small scratches, and Tony kissed her as they both finished together once again. She had been so right by letting her have her way; he would never forget her, ever.

Time passed, and Michelle rolled to her side and then crawled toward him again on the king-sized bed; she wasn't done, but then she remembered the time. The massive open room had windows all the way around it, and the bed was in the center. They were making love under the stars and lights of the city. This was their first time, and she had promised something so special, and she felt she had delivered. The clock on the wall had only five minutes left till midnight; pleasure had to end. Tony was breathing hard when she crawled on top of him again. He tried to stop her, but she wasn't having it. She began again, pinning him down once more, and he submitted again; moments later, he started to climax again, and she cried out.

"I AM YOURS, AND YOU ARE MINE!" she screamed out in her own climax and then fell on top of him, and her lips met his for a moment.

After the kiss, Michelle's thorn then sliced deeply into his aorta with a swipe of her long tongue, and she felt his blood practically spray into her mouth because he was climaxing too. It was only a pure aphrodisiac for her, and her thorn slid inside, and she began to drink deeply of the passion and love laced in his essence for her first time. Michelle's skin pulsated softly as she fed, and she could feel Tony's doing the same, and she partook in his life force. Just then she felt his soul for the first time, his very soul, the only one she had ever professed love like this for, and she sensed his willingness to give that to her too. But Michelle stopped and closed the wound; she wouldn't take that. She had taken enough from him, and she refused her demonic side utterly. She fell into his arms as her tongue resettled in her mouth, and she almost passed out. Suddenly a reddish light bathed the room, and she nearly cried out in joy. She had done it! The aura was her sign, and only she could see it! Then she felt overwhelming lust flood over her; it was hers! It was the emotion that had driven him to her now reversed when the aura was created, and it was part of it now. It affected her deeply, and she wanted to create him right then and now, but she had to wait; both of them were too weak. She reminded herself how much she loved him and to be patient. Tony had passed out, and Michelle checked his heart to make sure—fast but strongly beating—and smiled again. He was alive! She tried to get up but fell to the mattress again and back on top of him. As if on cue, Tony's arms wrapped around her in a loving embrace. He said only three words as he passed out again, "I…love… you…" It was said like a sweet whisper, but she heard it and smiled.

Michelle absolutely believed him, and then her world went dark too. Together both of them passed out in each other's arms in love. The lust radiating around the room had almost no effect on her because the love in her heart was enough to hold it at bay. As her world darkened, Michelle realized that this love was real; if it could hold her lust back, this love could be the defining moment of their lives now too, and she shut her eyes slowly.

Hours passed by, and the night waned, and Michelle was the first to wake, still being held softly by her lover. She glanced around the room and felt the lust in the air lulling her back to him. She felt almost drunk the closer she was to him. She then realized the time; it was so early. There was no way she could leave here without risking death. Michelle wriggled out of Tony's grasp and wobbled to her feet, but she could hardly walk. She had to get to the bathroom; there were no windows in there. Sleeping in the bathtub would be better than burning, but she wasn't going to make it; she was going to fall. In the gradually fading darkness, she saw the shades on the windows. She half walked and half staggered to the shades and hit the button on the wall, and they slid closed, blotting out all the light in the room. She slumped down and fell to a sitting position upon the wall. She tried to get up but just couldn't; she was so spent, and her legs had just failed. She had no strength left from the moments they had shared, and with the coming of dawn, she was done; there was a good chance she was about die. After finding true love, Michelle was going die. *How beautiful,* she thought. She began to slump over, and something stopped her from falling to the carpets on the floors. She forced her eyes open, and Tony had her in his arms. He was as weak as she was, but he carried her back to the bed. She put her arms around his neck as he walked. He laid her down softly and pulled the heavy blankets around her. He then slipped in next to her, and her hands met his skin as she put her head on his chest. Michelle pulled the blankets over her head and passed out, and Tony followed suit. She could only hope the shades and blankets kept out the killing sun. Together they shared a bed for the first time, and as Michelle drifted away, she wondered how many Immortals have ever shared their bed with a mortal before in the coming dawn. Blackness closed in around her, and she fell into the deepest sleep of her life with her lover. Tomorrow night would be here soon enough, and under the covers, blue flames wreathed her eyes as love-filled sleep lulled her mortal soul to calm.

15

CHAPTER

In Times Square, the sun had finally set, and Michelle woke as night settled in, letting out a short sigh of relief; she was alive. Thankfully Tony hadn't moved all day, and she pulled the blankets away slowly and saw the shades were dark, then she blew out another deep sigh of relief. Tony had saved her life this morning—she was sure of it. Had he not shielded her, she would be dead now. This just affirmed her belief that he was meant for her, and this was right. She was going to let him sleep, and she had a reservation for this room for a few nights. Tony was going to stay here and rest and relax; he needed it from her constant feedings on him. She would see him in three days' time, and he would say goodbye to the world of mortals forever. Michelle stood softly and looked for any remnant of her clothes she had been wearing, but they were scattered around the now dark room. When the door had closed, they couldn't get out of them fast enough. Then she realized, why should she care if Tony was here, and if she couldn't be in the nude with her lover, what was the point of any of this? Once on her feet, she could feel the lust in the room calling out to her; she wanted him again. But Michelle shook her head and told herself to remember the love they shared, don't give into the lust they had for each other. She walked over to the en suite and tiptoed inside, shutting the door behind her. Then she turned the light on then off again—too bright this early. She started to shower hoping it wouldn't wake him. Michelle turned the hot water all the way up. Immortals enjoy heat so much, and she stepped into the large shower stall. She stood still, allowing her body to soak up the hot water, loosing up her sleep-weary body. It felt so good, and most days she couldn't get it hot enough to her liking. The glass steamed up, and Michelle leaned her head back, letting the water run through her long dark hair. She had her eyes closed for a moment and was just starting to really relax when the door of the shower opened suddenly. Through the hazy steam, she saw Tony standing there as nude as she was.

"Good evening, lover, hope you—" she began to say but never got to finish.

Tony stepped into the shower quickly and closed the door behind him. Her back hit the wet tile wall, and his lips met hers as lust ran through her body rampantly. The water ran down the both of them, and the heat didn't bother him one bit. From the steamy glass from the outside of the shower, soon Michelle's hand slammed on the glass and then slid down it. If this was to be her eternity, she could get very used to this; he was incredible.

Once the shower was over and they had finished drying off, Michelle asked Tony to sit with her for a moment. They were both in white fluffy hotel robes, and they took a seat on the heated veranda that was off the side of their room. She straightened the towel holding her hair and then kissed him once quickly.

"Listen to me, sugar, I booked this room for the next three days. So, I want you to stay here. You've been sick, and you still look weak too. I want you to heal up here. Relax, watch TV, have room service, do whatever it is you like, and ask for anything you want. But I would really like you to stay here though. I've got to go out of town for the next day or so, but I promise you with everything I hold dear, I will call you in three days or less, but here," she said, leaning back and relaxing in the moonlight.

Tony looked back at her and sat up a little. It was true he hadn't been feeling like himself, but did it warrant him staying cooped up for the next seventy-two hours? He had a few things he had to take care of at home. He wanted to take a moment to talk to his mother and his sister. Tell them both about Michelle and about falling in

IN THE NAME OF SIN

love. He also wanted them to meet her too; he was a little worried, but he was certain Michelle would love them both. Still, he had a few things he needed to get done too before he missed the spring semesters at the schools he had to apply to.

"What if I don't want to stay here? I've got a few things I need to see to myself. Just take me with you if you wanna keep tabs on me so bad. Why put me in here and leave me alone after last night?" he asked, still a little confused after the night they just had.

Michelle loved that he wanted to be around her right now, but they couldn't; she was fighting for control even now. She could see his pale-reddish aura still, and it was calling to her—no, *demanding* her to take him yet again. The longer they sat together, the harder it was for her to resist. Even during the shower, she felt her tongue split in her mouth a few times; she desperately wanted to feed on him again. She hadn't lusted for anything like this before in so long. Better to protect him and let him regain strength by relaxing here in one of this hotel's premier suites.

"I understand, and I would love nothing more than to take you with me, sugar, but I can't. It's family business, and it can't be avoided. Like I said, a day and half to two days tops. I promise this isn't some ploy or something else for me to ditch you. I care about you so damn much, and you've been so sick, and you woke up weak and sickly today again. You didn't think I saw you dry-heave a few times in the en suite, and you still look pale now. You stay here, please rest, and I will call you soon, I promise. When I get back, I'm coming right here to get you, then I'm not letting you go, ever," she said, getting up because she needed to make space between them. He was so intoxicating to her. "But please promise me you'll stay right here in the hotel. They will supply you with anything you need, want, or desire. I've even got some nice comfy clothes coming up soon for you in moments," she said, walking toward the en suite again.

Tony sat back again because he was so tired. "How do you know this hotel will give me anything I want? And what about my job, Michelle? I've got to go back to work at some point," he asked her with a weak laugh, but she stopped and looked back at him.

"One, because my family owns it, and if they upset you, they upset me. They don't want to do either. Two, as of now, Tony, you are the most important guest they have here too. Now when it comes to your job, forget it. I want you to call and quit tonight. I will not have you working in that horrid place as long as you have me in your life. If you have a need, you ask me from now on, sugar," she said back adamantly and began walking again. She still needed to have distance from him before she'd snap.

Eventually he agreed to stay as long as he could call home and tell them he'd be home in a few days. Michelle agreed, and the knock at the door signaled their clothes had arrived. It was time for her to go—and soon; she really needed to. The lust was getting too strong now. An hour or so later, Michelle had gotten dressed and had a few of her "girls" or entourage come up to fix her hair and makeup and see to her needs. Cassie, Stephanie, Amanda, Ginger, and Lucy, unknown to Tony, were all Immortals that saw to Michelle when she called on them. Little did Tony know she did that to cloud the drawing aura swirling around the room too. Michelle could feel it; if she stayed any longer, she was going to crack, and none of these girls would be able to hold her back.

A little while later, she met him at the doorway, and he looked miserable because she was leaving, and Michelle looked amazing. Tony hugged her a bit, and the lust radiating from him was clouding her judgment even now. She really had to get away from him as much as she absolutely hated it. He was way too weak to take another round of feedings; he would never survive her and a fourth time right now. She walked out the door but told him that she had booked a massage therapist for him in about fifteen minutes, then she had his late breakfast being sent up in an hour. Last, she had a spa session for him in about four hours; finally, there was a woman named Janet at the front desk who was his personal assistant for the next three days. He was supposed to call her for anything he wanted or needed. Michelle kissed him quickly and said goodbye and then shut the door. She realized she couldn't set foot in that room again, or she'd kill him. Later tonight, he'd have another round of treatments with an acupuncturist that more than likely would burn sage in the room, and the smoke would keep her from there for at least two days. Tony was safe as long as he stayed in that room from anything in the city, especially her. She arrived at the lobby and said goodbye to the girls. Michelle then suddenly stopped Cassie from leaving by putting her hand on her shoulder.

"You're my most trusted and oldest friend, Cassandra. I want this hotel watched. If he tries to leave, stop him, subtly. Let me know at once if he does. If someone tries to harm him, kill them, and once more, let me know immediately—rouse me from slumber, I don't care," she said to her in a very serious tone and look in her eyes.

Cassie nodded back to her, bowing her head too. "Yes, my mistress, it will be as you ask. No harm will come to our future sovereign, and I will watch him and give my life if I must see him safely back to you," she said back just as serious, and Michelle let out a laugh.

"Seriously, Cassie, it's me, and don't call me *mistress*, I hate that, and you know it," Michelle said back annoyed, and Cassie just grinned back sarcastically and began to leave.

"You know I just do it to get you upset, but worry not, I'll check up on him daily, and if anyone tries to enter that room, I'll see to it. I've got a condo not far from here I use for meetings and such. If I have to, I'll bring him there, and you can meet us later on that night. I'll get you the address if you need it. No one will find him until you find us first," Cassie said and headed for the doors of the hotel.

Then Michelle met with Janet quickly and, after a brief chat, made her realize he was not to leave that room alone or especially the building under any circumstances for the next three days. The woman nodded slowly at first then snapped out of it again. She gave Michelle her personal cell number, and she planned on checking in with her later and especially Tony very soon too. Then the limousine picked her up and took her to the Factory, and now began waiting three days; and on the third night, her perennial loneliness would finally be lifted, she hoped.

Soon Michelle arrived somewhat on time at the club. She walked inside and headed right down to the Abyss, because she needed a stiff drink to clear her head, and she had to feed nightly too. Two nights would pass quickly, and on the third, she would try for the last time to create a prodigy of her own. Below, Elijah was waiting for her and then had to ask, seeing her a bit forlorn tonight.

"Well, I haven't seen you in three nights, and I do understand why too. Were you successful?" he asked, seeing Michelle ordering a drink and upset too.

Michelle nodded and tapped the bar looking for her usual; when the bartender brought it, she asked him for a shot of Stoli on the side. Elijah watched her down it fast and then take a long sip of her drink. She then asked for another shot, and Elijah just watched her and couldn't understand why she was so upset.

"Well, I see it wasn't easy on you. You can still back out of this, Michelle, simply don't go to him on the third night, and the process will fail with no jeopardy to you," he said, watching the bartender slide her another shot.

She then looked back at him and shook her head while taking another long drink off her glass. "Never, he will be mine, it's tough this time, Elijah, the aura calls to me even here. Not as loudly as it does when I'm near him, but faintly. But I want to give him two nights and a day to recover before I deliver the fourth and my dark gift," she said, downing the shot again and setting the glass on the bar.

Elijah set his glass on the black stone bar and asked for another then sat about a chair apart from her. "Very wise, my young prodigy, to allow him to recover. This will only improve your chances of success later on. So you took him home?"

Michelle shook her head again and drained her own glass, sliding it down the bar. "No, I left him in a suite in Midtown closer to Times Square. He will be safe there and able to recover fully on the mini vacation I put him on. One of his treatments I scheduled will use sage most likely. That will keep me from the room in case I break down mentally."

Elijah raised a brow in disbelief seeing her wisdom in this. He couldn't believe someone as rash as Michelle had been lately had thought this out so well in advance. "Well done, Michelle, the sage smoke should last a day and half tops and will keep you from the room as long as he doesn't vent the smoke out with fresh air though."

Michelle picked up her drink and took another long sip. "He's on the top floor. With the exception of the small veranda, the windows don't open. I planned for all contingencies this time. If I'm going to succeed this time, I cannot be rash right now," she said back but still seemed so upset too.

Elijah stood and leaned on the bar now. "So why do I see a miserable Immortal like he's dead already?"

Michelle turned in her seat and then picked up her glass again. "Because I miss him terribly right now. I want him with me, but I cannot have my fondest wish for another two nights. And as much as I do realize how short that is for me, the minutes drag by, let alone the hours. After having him at my side for three nights, I only realized how long these years have been. I feel lost, Elijah, like I have nothing right now."

Elijah then stepped closer to Michelle and put his hand on her shoulder. "As surly, moody, discontented, and eccentric as you can be, you have been a good prodigy. I would think you will be just as good of a creator too. Take these nights and celebrate his upcoming rebirth like you're supposed to. Remember how I celebrated yours. Don't see it as despair, see it as a time to both plan and look forward to. In other words, Michelle, think of it as a reason for happiness, and celebrate those long years you waited for. You're about to have untold centuries of company."

Michelle looked up and finally grinned a bit; it was time for her to celebrate his upcoming rebirth, and her days as a solitary Immortal were over. She saw it as a reason for two nights of hell-raising because soon she would have to set an example for her prodigy. The Factory was about to get one more taste of Michelle Victoria Du'Pree in all her glory, the likes it hadn't seen in decades.

A few hours later, Michelle had the entire club whipped into a frenzy of celebration. When most of the Immortals found that another royal blood elder very well could be joining them soon, all they did was congratulate her and wish her luck on the upcoming prodigy to her house. No one could know it was her that was the soon-to-be creator, but it still made for such a spectacle that encompassed every floor in the place. The third floor had easily overflowed, and the large screen on the fourth floor and sound system played the music from the third! It had been so long since every floor was packed. The line outside stretched four blocks now, but they were at capacity, and the fire marshal had been by twice now, and even he couldn't get in for an inspection. Michelle had fed well tonight, almost too well. Her experiences with feeding upon Tony for three nights allowed her to better judge when to stop before leaving her victim a visible wreck. She was up to her sixth, and she flopped into the couch in the Abyss next to Elijah and put her head on his shoulder.

"Thank you, Elijah, I needed this tonight," she said with a wide smile and finished her latest glass of wine and tossed it to the table.

He swirled his drink and looked down at her. "You're most welcome, and you've garnered so much business here tonight for the club, I thank you. Just keep the fire marshal out of here tonight."

Michelle laughed out loud and called for another drink. "Oh, he won't be a problem tonight, I took care of that. He's quite drunk on floor two, he just needed a little mental push."

Elijah spit out his drink and began to laugh out loud. "You are on a roll tonight, aren't you?" He then spied something and began to get up. "Please excuse me, but I think I see something that needs my immediate attention," he said and walked off, and Michelle watched her creator wade into a group of young Immortal women. She smiled widely for him because Elijah needed this too.

Meanwhile, back at the hotel in Midtown, Tony had just finished his spa treatment that Michelle had arranged for him. It was relaxing, but getting his nails manicured still bothered him; he honestly hated it. The people at the spa were insistent that Ms. Du'Pree was adamant about every treatment. Tony had never felt so relaxed before, between the long massage before, then a meal that had something to do with roasted quail eggs that he couldn't remember the names of, but it was fantastic. He then headed down to the spa and afterward, and now he felt so damn good. Much better than this evening when he woke up sick, that's for sure. When he arrived at his room, his next appointment was waiting for him, and the acupuncturist introduced himself. At first, he wasn't interested, but then he remembered the things had read about it for joints and muscles

IN THE NAME OF SIN

that would help him in a martial arts way, so he decided to give it a try. As he lay down on the table, he watched the acupuncturist light incense and begin the therapy. Tony then asked what he was burning in the small braziers, and he had said, "Sage, to help cleanse the room and bring about healing." The therapy lasted quite a while and surprisingly didn't hurt much at all. When he was done, he was informed his hot tub was at temperature; and once he had soaked for a bit, his lunch was delivered. Obviously Michelle had chosen it and was brought in and left on the cart. The hot mineral water helped to relax away fatigue, and he only wished he was sharing this night with her. He had called home and said he had gone upstate to check out a college with a few friends and that he'd be home in about three days. Then Tony called his job, and it felt so good to just up and quit over the phone; he just hoped he wouldn't regret it later. Afterward, he leaned back in the hot mineral water and closed his eyes. As he let his mind begin to wander, Tony found out he was longing for Michelle. It felt like something was calling to him to go and find her. He knew that he missed her terribly, but never had he felt like this about a girl. He had no explanation, but it was like he was getting upset being parted from her. Tony went back to relaxing again, trying to let go of this feeling he was having. Michelle was right, he needed this, and it was helping too. Little did he know what he was feeling was the lust they both shared right now for each other. The feeling he had was that he wanted Michelle to take her fourth from him so he could be with her forever. Even though Tony had no idea, right now Michelle was very dangerous when it came to him; she was desiring him just as much, and if she got anywhere near him right now, she would never resist him.

CHAPTER 16

Back downtown, the party at the club was winding down, and it was almost closing time as well. Michelle Du'Pree was walking through the Abyss and was greeted by even more guests and well-wishes from other dominant house of New York. On the far wall of the room was the Pyramid of Power, showing the other Immortal houses that had a say in the direction of New York. House Du'Pree sat at the very top of the pyramid for centuries, and the closer a house was to the top, the more direction they had. It's why all of the well-wishes came with smiles but also secret hopes of failure too. No one wanted to see House Du'Pree gain any more power than they had right now. Welcome to the world of the Immortals; everyone was supposed to be of one blood, but they would spill that blood as quickly as they could in order to garner more power. Michelle hurried past though. Elijah had called her to the office, and she was heading there as discreetly as she could. She finished with the well-wishes and thanks and quietly got in the elevator and rode to the hidden fifth floor. She stepped out of the elevator and called out Elijah's name, but suddenly something struck her hard, sending her spiraling down the hallway. Michelle landed on her back but recovered fast. She whirled around, claws bared, looking for a fight. Whoever it was, was strong, but she didn't care right now. Silently out of a wisp of smoke near her, Lady Anneke Elisabeth Du'Pree stepped out! She then punched her hard

IN THE NAME OF SIN

in the gut, and Michelle doubled over in pain. But Anneke grabbed her hair and drove her knee into Michelle's face, shattering her nose, sending her flying in the air. With an inhumanly swift move of her hand, she caught her like she was nothing. Then she flipped Michelle over in the air again and threw her through the door of Elijah's office. Michelle hit the floor and desk at once and tried to get up, but Anneke kicked her hard in the head, and a resounding crack rang out. She reached down and grabbed her again, dragging her to her feet and lifting her in the air before smashing Michelle through the heavy desk by her throat. Anneke wasted no time and kicked her over onto her hands and knees. She then screamed at her to get up, and Michelle had to comply because she had absolutely no will against her. As she got up, Anneke grabbed her headfirst and drove her head into the wall, smashing through the drywall, and Michelle fell again to the floor. Once again Anneke roared at her to get up but to stand still this time. She walked right up and grabbed her throat, again hauling her off the ground. Michelle struggled, but suddenly flames burst from Anneke's hand, burning her skin and face. She screamed in agony, but Anneke hardly cared, and she threw her across the room, smashing through a large bookcase.

Michelle put her hands on the floor to try to rise, but Anneke stepped on her hand hard. Then she kicked her in the gut once more as Michelle fell face-first to the floor among the broken wood and various objects scattered from the one-sided fight. A moment passed, and Anneke reached down again and grabbed her hair and hauled her to her feet once more. Michelle tried to fall, but Anneke screamed at her to stand. This is why she hated her so much; a long time ago, this witch had stripped her of her will against her. She then looked her right in her eyes, and Michelle spoke first in a very shaky voice.

"I'm so sorry, mistress...for the fight in the Abyss...a few nights ago." She was assuming that's what this was about.

Anneke sneered back at her then slapped her scorched face hard. "You think I even care about that? You should've killed the insolent Bael bitch! Elijah has been dealt with too. He shall never stay your hand again! And I don't care about the slaughter in Queens either. Why would I care about you killing a few scraggly mortals!

But what I do care about is you slumbering the day away with your new mortal at a hotel while you hold my precious bloodline in your fucking veins! Your lack of judgment disturbs me greatly, Michelle, after I told you to be PRUDENT, because if you had died in the sun in that hotel room, you cripple *my* house! Next time, show better judgement, or this moment of your fucking life will feel like a fond memory! Never threaten my house again, Michelle, do you understand me clearly this time?" Anneke snarled at her and grabbed her chin, looking her in the eyes. Michelle nodded, but Anneke scowled at her, "Speak it before I make you suffer again!" She roared at her, and Michelle answered fast.

"Yes…my…mistress," she said back weakly.

"Good, we have an understanding finally, after so many years," she said back snidely.

Without warning, she back-hand-punched her to the floor. Michelle looked up through the black blood on her face rapidly steaming away, only to watch Anneke step through a portal and vanish once more. She then crawled through the wreckage to the phone lying on the floor. She speed-dialed a number and waited a moment, then someone picked up.

"Help me…Elijah… I'm a wreck," she said, and then blackness closed in around her, and she fell facedown. It seemed the years of bad blood between Anneke and Michelle had just spilled over yet again.

A little while later, Michelle woke and felt like all of hell had beaten her. This wasn't the first time Anneke had done this, but this was definitely the worst by far. For so long, both Anneke and she never saw eye to eye. Across the room and near the door, Elijah knocked on the wall to get her attention. He had a red welt across his face from a nasty slap. He then slid something to her, and Michelle weakly picked it up and then dropped it, disgusted.

"I'm not drinking that shit, Elijah," she said back, but Elijah scowled back at her.

"You've got little choice now. The club is closed, you're a wreck, and you need to rapidly heal because I'm not getting anywhere near you right now either. It's also less than an hour till dawn. So, drink it!" he said back, lightly punching the wall.

IN THE NAME OF SIN

Michelle knew she had no choice and picked up the warm bag of Syn-Es.9, or Synthetic Essence, a horrible cocktail of blood plasma, proenzymes, and adrenaline, among other things. It was developed by one of their pharmaceutical firms in secret for moments just like this. Her thorn slit a hole in the top of the bag, and she upended the contents. The moment the sickly-looking orange fluid touched her tongue, she nearly gagged as the foul-smelling and disgusting warm liquid nearly made her wretch. To her it was like drinking fresh vomit. She finished the bag, and Elijah slid her another, and she felt like she was going to puke herself. Elijah watched her then frowned again because she wouldn't touch it.

"Don't do it, Michelle, keep it down and let it work, allow your-self to heal!" he said back loudly, now getting even more annoyed.

Michelle felt the disgusting liquid go to work, sating her craving to hunt and start the healing process. She picked up the next one in shaky hands and repeated the process and then howled in disgust and tossed the empty bag away.

"I'm…I'm going to…throw up," she said, grabbing her mouth, and she felt some of the foul-smelling liquid squirt through her fingers.

She swallowed hard and pulled her own vomit back down her throat. Elijah slid her the last bag, and Michelle nearly threw up again at the sight of it and pushed it away; just looking at it made her want to throw up right now. The stuff was horrible, and if she drank any more, she would puke. The warm gelatinlike fluid tasted so foul she would rather drink New York sewer water than that at the moment.

"I can't! I just can't, Elijah… I'm not drinking it again… I just fucking can't," she said back, but he insisted she did.

"You either drink it or I lock this door, and you can sleep in there, so fucking do it!" Elijah said, now getting angry about this.

Michelle complied and picked up the last bag and once again slit the top and upended the fluid and took down the last bag. She then dropped the empty bag and rolled over onto her back. She screamed out in disgust, but the foul-smelling and foul-tasting warm fluid went to work. Within a few minutes, she was sated, and her body had no more grievous wounds. Her clothes were trashed, but her body looked brand-new. She rolled to her side and dry heaved, and her long tongue slid out of her mouth, trying to shake off the disgusting taste. Elijah then stood up and walked into his devastated office. He righted and sat in the old chair as Michelle sat on the floor, with her knees to her chest, rocking in pain and disgust. Then he had to ask finally what caused the destruction of his office this time.

"What in fuck's sake did you do to piss her off this bad this time, Michelle? I told you she was still in the city. Believe me now, she can be here at any time?" he said, rubbing his cheek and jaw from being slapped before and then listening to Anneke's tirade about what happened with Iris.

She then told him about the morning in the hotel, and he shook his head, telling her it was not smart using a family hotel and doing that. Anneke probably stewed for hours before she got here. Michelle looked up at his face and saw the slap he had taken from the red handprint.

"She hit you too, huh?" she asked him, now feeling bad for her creator.

Elijah nodded back to her and seemed more annoyed than angry. "Seems the next time I ever go against the house, I'll get worse. I just tried to keep a body from turning up here or a war starting between Bael and Succubus Incubus castes. Who would've thought that was a bad idea?" he said back, just trying to forget about it. Anneke was mad about other things before that had even come up. When she arrived here late in the night, she was irate.

Now both of them were trapped in the club and had to spend the day here. Elijah let Michelle have the small bed in the lounge since she took a worse beating, and he would take the chair. Together neither of them would sleep well that day, but Michelle was now wondering if bringing Tony into this world was a good idea either. She had just had a large dose of reality when it came to this dark world in which she lived in. There were actions, and then there were consequences, and sometimes it felt like the consequences were a bit to the extreme. Still, what else was left, and could it get much worse than this, she began to wonder.

CHAPTER 17

Sometime in the early afternoon, Tony rolled over in bed and found it empty; he could smell Michelle but yearned to be with her now. It's like she was calling to him. The tender moments they had spent together only strengthened his love and desire for her. Just then the phone rang, shaking him from his thoughts, and he rolled back over to pick it up. It was the front desk about his lunch, and it was prepared, and they're asking if they could bring it up to him now. He agreed and decided to get out of bed and got dressed in another set of the comfortable clothes Michelle had bought for him here. A short while later, the cart was brought in, and it was swordfish steak with mixed vegetables. He had never even tried that before, like he could ever afford to either. The woman Janet told him that he had an appointment with a tailor for a new suit that Ms. Du'Pree wanted fitted today with her personal stylist present. Then he had another appointment to get his hair cut and trimmed by a hairdresser Ms. Du'Pree wanted brought in too. She then said the spa expected him shortly after that; he had steam bath and facial today too. Tony was beginning to think this was too much, but Janet was adamant about Ms. Du'Pree's wishes and said the tailor would be here within an hour or so from the Armani Exchange; they had quite a few styles to go over with him, and the stylist, then the fitting. She then left to let him eat, and Tony shook his head. Michelle was going over-the-top as usual.

Back at the Factory, the sun was still up, and Michelle rolled over in the old beat-up bed. She hated this room, and for good reasons too. Her last failure happened in here, and now she was so close to trying again while being forced to relive that horrible night. She rolled over again and tried to get comfortable, but she couldn't on the same bed her last friend had died on, thanks to her. She had to get back to sleep though, but the Synthetic Essence burned like acid in her chest, not to mention she couldn't get the disgusting taste out of her mouth either. The stuff was truly horrible, and she would have to feed a lot tonight to purge the rest of it out of her body. Her face and neck still hurt from the burns too. Why did she have to burn her too? It reminded her from her scars as a child; it felt like them too. She stared at the ceiling thinking of Tony and began to wonder if taking him to this world was worth it. She thought for a moment and then thought better to bring him to her and share their love forever than watch him be destroyed by ten thousand cuts of pain and agony the mortal world would give him. She knew all too well that pain; she had lived it. Michelle settled back into the uncomfortable bed and closed her eyes once more, hoping she was right this time.

In Midtown, Tony, on the other hand, had just finished yet another day of pampering that Michelle had set out for him. His fitting went well, and the style of suit he had chosen was more to his taste, and Michelle's personal stylist had finally approved, but nothing was cheap from Armani; and when he saw the bill, he nearly told them forget it. He couldn't believe it cost that much for a single suit. The spa was okay, but once again, he hated the facial but tried because Michelle wanted him too. Tomorrow he was to get up early for another round of the hot mineral bath; he then had to go back to the spa for another round of what he called Michelle messing with him, and if there was any waxing, he wasn't doing it this time. There was also another round with the tailor to check the fitting, and after his early dinner, he had a hairstylist named Lucy, who Michelle had used coming in for him. Lastly the car would be here at seven thirty to pick him up and take him to a location they were told by Ms. Du'Pree. Tony had no idea what she was up to but wondered, If she was going through this much trouble, was it worth it?

IN THE NAME OF SIN

Over in Downtown Manhattan, in Chelsea, the sun had finally set, and Michelle got up out of the horrible rickety old bed. From the office, she heard Elijah groan and knew he was awake too. She met him in the hall, and Michelle thought he looked no worse for wear. It was amazing what a day's sleep could do, even in discomfort and feeling sick from the horrible Synthetic Essence. She stretched once and then told him the bed was no better than the chair. Elijah then admitted it was time to fully update up here, and now there was a reason to. Michelle agreed and took out her nearly-dead cell phone and made one call to a car service to get them picked up and head over to their havens to get ready for tonight. Both of them hoped for a less-eventful night, but Michelle was going to have to do a lot of hunting; tomorrow was a big night, and she needed all the strength she could get.

That same night in Times Square, Tony rolled over again, took a look at the clock in his huge lavish room, and saw it was barely 2:00 a.m., and he couldn't sleep. Michelle's night owl hours were rubbing off on him, and he really missed her now. He had another massage before bed and a nightcap of chamomile tea, but it wasn't helping. Why hadn't she called him at all to let him know she was all right? He hadn't heard from her in just over twenty-four hours and wanted to know why. He was starting to wonder why she had packed his days with pampering activities as he sat up and gazed across the city skyline. He'd much rather do this with her instead of alone. He had a good mind to check out tomorrow and go home, but she had promised; and for as long as he had known her, she never lied to him about something like this. He was just lonely and missing the girl he finally told he loved a day ago. Tony grabbed the phone from his room and picked up his beat-up pager, found her number from a previous message, and dialed.

Back at the Factory, Michelle just finished with her sixth and had slipped through the hidden doorway. She wasn't using her abilities because she didn't want to have to hunt again tomorrow night. As she shut the door, her phone in her pocket began to ring and vibrate, and she took it out and answered a local number. Just then there was a voice on the phone that she missed so much!

135

"Michelle, please tell me this is your number?" Tony asked, and she moved away from the noise from the doorway to answer him.

"Sugar! It's so good to hear your voice, and yes, I know I forgot to call you. This business trip beat the crap out of me, literally," she said, still feeling the horrible beating Anneke had given her.

"Why is it so noisy? I can hardly hear you," he asked and sounded so lonely, and Michelle knew how that felt.

She then cursed under her breath. "I got home a little early tonight and decided to get a quick drink at the club before I headed back to SoHo. What are you doing awake though? You're supposed to have been very preoccupied today and even more busy tomorrow before the car comes to get you. It's why I didn't call, I thought you'd be asleep. I can't wait to see you, by the way, I want you to know that, and I miss you so much!" she said back, hoping he didn't suspect anything.

"If you're at the club, I can come down there now if you like," he said, and once again she cursed quietly.

"No, Tony, I just stopped in for drink, which I'm nearly done with to unwind, and I'm waiting for Elijah to finish up here too. I'm exhausted, and you're not done getting pampered like I instructed them to do. I'm not seeing you three-quarters done. You're going to have to wait till tonight so I can look my best for you too," she answered, walking down the stairs to the much quieter Abyss.

"I just miss you, is all, but why all of this pampering, as you call it? You didn't have to, and I saw the price of that suit too. I'm a little embarrassed right now," he said back, still missing her badly. And she knew why; she was the same exact way. They wanted to be together.

Michelle then walked just to the doorway that led into the Abyss; it's why she loved him so much. He didn't care about the money; he just wanted her and nothing more. This was her reason she had decided he was to be her one, her prodigy. Tony only cared about her and never cared about the money or her prestige she was about to hand to him.

"It's my treat to you, and you deserve it. You pamper me with your unconditional love, so I'm just returning the favor. Tomorrow night, I'm showing you off, because you took me off the market, and

I want every guy to be so jealous about that, not to mention every girl sad too because you're mine. So, get pampered, and I'll see you very soon, sugar. Trust me, I'm looking forward to it. I'm leaving very shortly also because Elijah is done here, and I'm going to SoHo to crash. I look horrible, and I'm not very much fun right now either. I'm actually a little bitchy, and I don't want you to see me like that, sugar," she said back, trying her best to sound tired.

"Okay, Michelle, I just wanted to say hello, and you've never given me a reason to distrust you before," he said back and sounded a little better.

But Michelle lightly bit her lip because she knew this was all a lie to cover up what she really was, and she hated it. "Tony, you're so very dear to my heart, and I would never try to harm you in any way. I would die if that happened. Do you remember what I told you? You are mine, and I am yours. I mean it with every drop of blood in my body. You can sleep soundly knowing that I am so looking forward to seeing you and only you tomorrow night, and I miss you just as much as you miss me. So, hang up the phone, sugar, have sweet dreams of us together, and tomorrow, I promise to make them all a reality. Do I not keep my promises to you?" she asked, feeling so confident again.

"Yes, you do," he said back, and she nodded with a smile.

They said goodnight, and Michelle hung up and then put her phone away. To her, this hurt; she hated keeping things from him. The sooner he was Immortal, the better in her eyes; no more lies, ever again—he didn't deserve that.

CHAPTER 18

The next night had finally come, the one Michelle had waited patiently for nearly three whole days. She was very confident that Tony would be revived nicely after the pampering and diet he'd been on. She had already heard from Janet that his lunch of bluefin tuna sashimi style was a hit, and he had enjoyed his hot-stone massage too. The spa, once again, not so much, and he hated the pedicure, which Michelle had thrown in there knowing very well it would annoy him, but if you couldn't have a bit of fun, then why even go through this at all. He had his third and final hot mineral water bath, and his suit had arrived on time. He was currently with her hairstylist Lucy and would be ready shortly. Everything when it came to his treatments and diet was designed to repair the damage she had caused with constant feedings for three nights. Michelle was very confident that he was in the best health he could be in three days' time. Cassandra had said the last few days had been quiet, and she had taken up residence in the hotel watching over Tony from afar but never getting too close either. He had eyes on him the whole time, and she had only left a few hours ago to see to a few things for Elijah.

Little did Tony know Michelle was in the car coming to get him. She was dressed so extravagantly in a very formal way. To her, it was another celebration, and they both needed to look their best together one last time. By tomorrow, the house should have another elder. Part of the reasons she had pampered him and dressed him so well was that this was the last night Antonio Willhiem would be seen again. She needed to get an idea how she was going to reform his new body. So she had everything "polished" to say to give her the best to work with. The limousine pulled up slowly to the front of the building, and Janet met Michelle outside and walked with her into the lobby. She assured her everything was exactly how she wanted it, and Tony should be down any minute, and her entourage had only left moments ago. Michelle nodded back then told her to put everything on the card on file and put an extra 30 percent for her and all the staff that helped. Janet nodded and took off to the front desk, but Michelle secretly wanted to know who was spying for Anneke here since she knew everything when she took that savage beating. When and if she ever found out who, she promised to return the favor tenfold, but that was best left for another night; tonight was too special to concern herself right now.

Just then Tony walked out of the elevator in his black Armani suit, with a white lightly striped shirt and no tie, just his collar loose. His shoes, a custom pair, were matte with shined heels and toes in all-black. His hair was done with gel and freshly cut, and he was clean-shaven only an hour ago by Michelle's personal hairstylist with a straight razor. Two women had to look twice as he walked past; his suit fitted him perfectly. He was unused to the idea of someone looking twice. Over his arm was a brand-new long leather coat that he slipped on slowly. He walked over to the front desk, and Janet told him he was all set and how handsome he was. Then, from behind, he felt hands run down his back and then wrap around him softly.

"Ah, you see, I'm so glad I waited, and you look dashing, I must say, and you smell fabulous too, how I've missed you," the voice said that he'd been longing for.

She let go, and Tony turned around and was amazed at her too. He'd never seen her in formal wear. She had on a custom black-and-silver Dior evening gown cut just right to show her curves off, and black wool wrap hung on her bare shoulders. Her hair was up, and her makeup was like a movie star's. Tony leaned down to kiss her, and she said no gently so as not to disturb her lipstick. She took him in then and then told him how they matched superbly. They walked out of the hotel hand in hand and over to the long stretch limo, and for once, Tony didn't feel out of place with her. Exactly what she wanted too. She had been trying to groom him early for the lifestyle of the New York elite; he would be part of it soon enough.

Once the car got going, Michelle handed Tony a bottle of Dom Perignon, and he couldn't believe his eyes; he knew how much this cost. She looked over at him and laughed, eyeing the bottle like it had diamonds in it or was made out of gold.

"Open it, silly. I bought it to celebrate our little reunion. I've missed you as much as you did me," she said with a wide smile as the limousine hit a little traffic.

Tony twisted the cork, and it popped but held on to it. Michelle nodded in approval; she found it very refined, and she took out two crystal glasses for them. She held one then the next, and Tony set the bottle back in the ice bucket, and Michelle handed him a fine crystal champagne flute. They sipped for a moment, and then she told him the driver was taking the long way back, so they had time to get reacquainted. Michelle was still in awe of how handsome he was. He was polished just as she had asked for, and already, she had grand ideas about his creation.

"I do like your new look and especially your suit. You picked well, and it's going to look amazing on my floor in a little while," she said with a playful giggle and sipped her glass.

Tony looked right at her bewildered then asked, "You know how much this suit costs, correct?"

But she then continued to laugh at his reaction. "Of course, I do, and it's only a suit, Tony, and it can be replaced. Just like I could care less if you tore my new evening gown to get me out of it privately for a moment of passionate lovemaking, because it too can be replaced. I'm an aggressive woman, Tony, and you should know that by now. When I want something, most times, I get it, and if I want you to tear my new gown off of me, then just do it. It's only money, you know, and that too can be replaced," she said back, taking another sip of her glass gently.

IN THE NAME OF SIN

"It's only money to you, Michelle, but when you grow up without it, you learn to respect what you've got," he said back, a bit annoyed at her callousness.

She then set her glass down but had to relax; there was another time for that story. "You won't have that problem either after tonight too, by the way," she said back, quickly trying not to get upset right now.

Tony then looked right at her as she looked out the window as the car drove on. "Okay, what's that supposed to mean, Michelle?" he snapped back, now getting annoyed.

"Nothing, I don't want to upset you, sugar, I want you to be happy. After tonight, I'll tell you everything, I promise. You know me and my little surprises and how much I love them. I promise you not only will you be surprised but your days of worry will be over very soon. Now I love you, and as long as you love me, then you never need to worry again, ever," she said back with a smile and then picked up her glass again.

Tony wasn't sure what she was up to, but if he knew her, it was simply over-the-top. Meanwhile, Michelle was once again wrestling for control being this close to him again. The aura was drawing her to him, and all she wanted to do was take him now and have him. Michelle felt her tongue split a little in her mouth in anticipation. She wanted to give in to the sweet lust he was weaving unknowingly around the car, but she kept telling herself, *Soon enough*. The moment was at hand, but just a bit longer, and that sweet essence would be hers again soon. She could practically taste it right now on her lips.

At the club, Michelle was never more than a few feet from Tony at a time. She was cordial and polite, greeting people, with such a gleeful demeanor that it even shocked him a few times. Her arm most times was in his, and like she said, she showed him off like her newest trophy. Even Elijah was quite impressed on how refined he looked, and Michelle's little private vacation had done wonders for Tony. The first two hours, Michelle was all about getting around the entire place quickly, but things changed as the night wore on a bit longer. Now all she wanted to do was get out of the club badly, and it was because mentally she was breaking from the aura. She had other ideas, and when she whispered in his ear, Tony agreed right away.

"Let's get out of here," she whispered sensually into his ear then drew his earlobe briefly into her mouth with a playful tug.

After Michelle had said that, Tony was a little relived; the club was filled with the rich and elite of Manhattan, and he was an average guy from Queens. As polished and refined as he looked, he felt he didn't belong. Michelle, on the other hand, was finding tougher to resist her prodigy-to-be as the night wore on. The aura around him called to her, and the more she tried to ignore it, the harder it got to resist him. She had to leave, and now, before temptation became too much for her to resist any more. When the car pulled up, they both got in, and she slammed the door, and immediately she was practically on top of him straddling him. She looked up from the back seat and at the driver and told him to drive fast to her place in SoHo. Michelle wasn't waiting anymore; she wanted him, and she could resist no more.

Once they arrived at Michelle's SoHo flat, she told the driver he could leave. Then Michelle led Tony inside and up the short stairs to what looked like a small place in SoHo but turned out to be a very large suite when they got inside. It was tastefully decorated from what he saw then, because Michelle grabbed him, and he was up against the wall so fast with her lips on his. He dropped his jacket to the floor, and Michelle, with one tug, opened his brand-new shirt by sending the buttons skipping across the floor. She dropped her wrap and walked up the small three stairs and to the hallway entwined with him. She then aggressively led him down the hall and then dove into his arms like before at the hotel. They made their way down the hallway stopping every foot or so, kissing the entire time. She kicked open the door to her bedroom, and together they crashed into the bed. Michelle began to pull both his suit jacket and shirt off, and when she did, she tossed them to the floor like she said she would. She then got on top of him and put his hands on her back. Tony tried to begin to take off her gown, but she wasn't having it and pinned him back down.

IN THE NAME OF SIN

"Like I said before, sugar, do it, rip it," she moaned, and then she put his hands on her back again with a wide smile on her lips and desire in her eyes.

With a pull of his hands, her beautiful gown tore, and it made her let out a resounding sigh as the expensive gown tore open. She wasn't kidding when she said that when she wanted something, she got it. Michelle fell atop him and opened his new pants with a simple tug, and before Tony could say a word, he fell backward again as Michelle began with fellatio. Tony let out a long sigh, and then it felt like his spine melted; whatever she was doing felt fabulous. She had promised to make his waiting worth it, and now once again, she had delivered. Meanwhile, what Tony didn't know was Michele had a split tongue and knew how to use it for pleasure.

A few hours later, it was getting close to midnight, and Michelle had had Tony a few times now and was only looking for more. A Succubus could be nearly insatiable, and Michelle knew she was pushing Tony's mortal limits now. But she felt his pleasure had to be right where she wanted it and began to prepare herself. This was the hardest part of creating a new elder, the fourth time. She put her hands on his chest and began to pleasure him again, but this time, she fell forward onto his chest. She then thought to herself, *I'm sorry, my love, if this hurts, but it must be done.* Then her tongue split, and her sharp thorn drilled hard into his chest, burrowing in deeply. Michelle felt it when it cut into his dense heart, and Tony winced in pain, but she held him down now with inhuman strength. She felt her thorn slip into his heart, and then her smaller fangs clamped down, locking her thorn in place. She began to feed directly from where his soul sat, and once more, lust-filled essence fed her body so well; she had craved it for days. Tony squirmed a bit, but she held him down again, only harder this time. In her mind, as she drank, she kept saying, *Submit to me, my love, let me have it, Tony. If you fight, it could be a disaster for us both.* And she began to stroke his head lovingly, trying to soothe him. She continued to feed softly, and he calmed, and his arms fell to the side as he submitted to her. As fast as Michelle could, she opened an artery in her wrist with her claws and rubbed the bloody wound on his lips.

Drink, my love, drink, but spill not a drop, she thought, and his lips fluttered upon her wrist ever so gently. She began to feed again but sped up, and she felt his sweetest essence flow to her. But it was so tantalizing because there was so little left, because he was close to death. Suddenly Michelle felt more suction on her wrist, and she smiled with glee. Once again, she thought to herself, *That's it, take from me as I take from you. We must share everything, my love. Take what you like.* But Michelle watched like a hawk as Tony drank, and when he shifted, a drop of blood ran down her arm. This time she used her other hand to wipe it up with her finger and then put the finger upon her long tongue, and it vanished. She went back to feeding, and suddenly her body began to freeze up. Her heart stopped, and she couldn't move, and her thorn let go and retracted into her mouth. Then the aura died around Tony, and something tore free inside of her. It flowed out of her heart and through the wound on her wrist and into him. Michelle felt Tony still drinking, but she couldn't move; she could only call out to him.

"Enough, my love, enough. Let me go. We now belong to each other in all things. We truly belong to each other now, but let me live too! ENOUGH!" she cried out with her body frozen in place.

With that, Tony stopped, and then he groaned and fell to the side as darkness suddenly enveloped his entire body as she fell to her side. Michelle got her feeling back throughout her body but was so weak, but she had to rise again. She placed her hands upon him and began to remold his likeness to her desires, changing everything about him. It took time, but once she was satisfied, she fell to the side yet again, utterly spent. Tony breathed in deeply, and Michelle put her lips on his. She wanted his first breath as an Immortal to be hers forever. She then fell to the side again and cried out in absolute glee. They had done it; her long nights of loneliness were over. Best yet, she loved him dearly. She crawled slowly to him and put her head upon his newly formed chest as the darkness receded slowly from his new body. She felt the blackness closing in, and she was about to pass out, but as she did, she said one more thing.

"Sleep well, my beautiful and beloved Zackarias, I shall see you soon, my love," she said softly and then passed out as flames wreathed her eyes.

They were of one blood, one life, and one soul; because as they drank, they shared everything precious they had, he was her prodigy now and forever. A part of her soul now resides in him, and a part of his soul had just finished settling in her heart. Michelle smiled widely as her body shut down; she could feel the warmth of his soul in her heart that lulled her to sleep. As Michelle faded away, another set of flames burst forth from her new creation.

EPILOGUE

Meanwhile in Forest Hills, Queens, Elijah Du'Pree was sitting in a black Mercedes-Benz in front of very nice house on a corner lot. He had just stopped here after the gathering at the club to meet someone. Mason Therew had become a problem a while ago, and he was one of Michelle's contacts in the office of the mayor of New York City. It seemed Mason, a middle-aged man, had a weakness for cute naïve girls; and when it came to Michelle, she could exploit that for years. He was married, had a wife, a fifteen-year-old daughter, and his elderly mother lived with him too. Elijah had made the trip here to try to talk some sense into him before he decided to do something rash. Information had been leaked from his office, and when it was leaked, Anneke had used that leak to land a lucrative contract with the city. She had easily gotten her hands on quite a few buildings she had her eyes on, and she was going to renovate them and then sell them back to the city. The deal would net her millions, but the information had been taken from Mason's desk all right— by Michelle. She had used one of her illusions to disguise herself as an office girl, Trisha, and gotten Mason drunk at dinner. Later they headed back to his office to use it to make love. Michelle had gotten a fine meal out of him and then copied the files she needed to give Anneke the inside edge on the buildings. She had put in the right bids, and Mason's good friends lost the contracts he was supposed to make millions on. Now he was threatening to go to the press because the police were a waste of time when it came to a Du'Pree. Elijah had come here to talk sense into him and to offer him a small job as an informant in the mayor's office, but he had refused and told him to leave. So Elijah was sitting in the car waiting, and only moments ago, Cassie, or Cassandra, had walked up to the front door of the house and knocked. When Mason opened the door, she leveled him with a single punch to the face and walked inside shutting the door behind her. That was five minutes ago, and now Elijah was looking to leave, but Cassie had to get the information Mason had first. Suddenly the phone rang in the car, and Elijah looked down at the number and picked it up fast.

"Good evening, Anneke, and what pray tell has you calling me so early? I have that little chore you asked Cassie and I to handle well in hand, if that's what you wish to know? I do think your little example you taught Michelle was a bit on the harsh side, but she did believe the slap you gave me, if that helps," Elijah said to her as he looked over at the house again.

"Oh, no, Elijah, I have no doubt that will be handled even though I asked Michelle to do it before. I do realize she has been quite distracted for the last few days even though I had to teach her a brief lesson about rationality throughout it. No, it takes time to create a new prodigy, and I have no doubts this time my daughter shall be successful. I do think we shall soon be greeting a new member of our house. I realize the example was harsh, but Michelle never excelled when subtlety was used before," Anneke said back in a joyful tone at the moment.

"I still think this is very dangerous, Anneke. Michelle has been volatile for a long time, and only thanks to Cassandra has she been that much less lately. You were told a long time ago that it was a bad idea to consider her. Now you're going to trust her choices because of why, may I ask. In recent years, some have been…poor, to put it lightly," Elijah said back to her as he glanced over at the house again.

"Well, that's only been like that the last forty years or so, and yes, she was a handful too after her perfect companion was lost. But Cassie has done wonders with her and continues to do so. You must understand, Elijah, when Michelle finds her prodigy, he will be her perfect choice, and through him, he will help to control her once more. Just like her perfect surrogate did for all those years after her creation. When you met her so long ago in France, she even convinced you of her great worth. Don't doubt yourself now, my prodigy, not when we are so close to having everything perfect again. You will see, through her prodigy, Michelle will once more become an important and infallible part of this house again. I've had high hopes for years, soon the struggles with her will be well worth the effort. We will finally have our sovereign, and then our house will become all we had envisioned so long ago. He's the key, and through him, all things will be possible, just like I said before about Michelle when you agreed to take her as yours," Anneke said to him, and suddenly four shots from a .45 rang out from the house he was parked in front of.

"That will remain to be seen, Anneke. Michelle has had more than a rough patch in her life. She nearly tore this house apart at one point a few times. Your actions didn't help either. Now I have to go, and if I know Cassie, she has just finished with our mayor's office problem and made it look like a murder suicide. We will talk more about this later on. I do see great quality in the young man when I met him, but this life can change someone, and sometimes not for the better, example Michelle," Elijah said and started up the Mercedes and put it in gear.

"I tell you now, Elijah, Michelle's prodigy will be the one to utterly transform this house into something of greatness. I have such faith in her, even though we are at such odds. Her life is about to change utterly. She will become the consort she once was," Anneke said back and then hung up the phone fast.

From the front of the corner house, Cassie walked out quickly and took off a set of latex gloves off her hands, depositing them in her jacket pocket. She opened the door to the car and sat down, tossing a single folder to the floorboards, and then shut the door as Elijah drove off. He knew what had happened, and Cassie had just executed an entire family in that house. It's how Anneke sent a clear and concise message to others who dealt with her and House Du'Pree. If you decided to betray her, then not only would you die, but your entire family would follow suit. Cassie had just shot Mason, his wife, his daughter, and his mother too. She had left the gun there, and now it looked like Mason Therew had murdered his family and then killed himself. It was the price for doing business with Anneke; there was always a price. She never told anyone all the details about anything, and not only was Elijah concerned about Cassie, who looked a little disturbed at what she had just did. He was always wondering more and more why Anneke was so sure Michelle, who had failed a few times to make a prodigy, would be successful this time. He was also curious why she was so interested and sure he would be something so special. As Elijah drove from the house in Forest Hills, it seemed like the shadows darkened, and the blackness got even more dense as he turned toward Manhattan again.

AN EXCERPT FROM PART 2 OF *IN THE NAME OF SIN*

Part of him wished he had asked Michelle to stay behind too. Her empathic senses would tell her if this bastard was lying to him or not. Still, it was best to leave her out of this for now; she had other problems that needed her immediate attention. Elijah then moved so fast it startled even Raul and looked him right in the eyes. With his gaze, Elijah had him under his ability of mind domination, and then he smiled widely, seeing Raul's eyes glaze over. After a moment, Elijah realized he was fully in his grasp and then sat back down.

"Now, this is the only prototype, or is there more? Is the schematic really on this chip, or have you lied to me like you have quite a few others? Speak truthfully and quickly too," he said, and Raul's eyes never even blinked.

"That's a fake, the real one is in my home, in Brooklyn, and the schematics are on the real one. The safe is in the floor of my bedroom under the rug near the bed. The combination is fifteen, thirty-three, six. The printout in the safe, that is the correct working schematics. The ones I gave you are close but not complete in the least," Raul said to him and lolled his head to the side a little as Elijah now scowled again.

"Good, very good, now give me your keys and wallet too," Elijah said to him, and Raul put them both on the table, and Elijah picked them up and then walked over to put them on the bar.

After a moment of watching, Raul seemed to be lost, but Elijah walked over to him, and with a swift move of his hand, he slammed his head across the table. Raul fell to the floor, now knocked from the small trance Elijah had put him in. He shook his head and was dazed as blood ran down his head from the vicious strike Elijah had delivered to him. Suddenly something wrapped around Raul's neck and tightened just as fast. He began to thrash because he could breathe now. When he looked over, Elijah's right arm had become a tentacle, like an octopus's! Raul was so stunned he tried to grab it to pull it off him, but Elijah picked him up and then slammed him through the table face-first. Cassie came running to the room, but when she got there, she stopped; the patron of House Du'Pree had this well in hand.

"So, you thought you'd rob me and then move on, hmm? I knew all about you, Raul Corstra, and how many you've ripped off, but most of the technology you have is sound this time. Now that I've got what I wanted, I don't need you anymore. Too bad, you, on the other hand, have stolen your last amount of money from anyone. Five million was a small investment to get to this. Goodbye, Raul, and maybe no one ever told you, don't rip off a Du'Pree. Cassandra has been keeping up on you the whole time, you little worm," Elijah said as his grip tightened around Raul's neck again.

Suddenly another tentacle formed on Elijah's left arm and grabbed a hold of Raul's foot. Cassandra watched on but stayed back. Elijah could augment his body how he wished, and soon he had picked up and lifted Raul into the air. With a fast pull of the two tentacles, Elijah ripped out Raul's spinal cord from his body with a sickening tear and a gory shower of blood, then he tossed both the body parts aside like nothing. He snapped the tentacles once, and then they reformed into his arms once more. He walked over to the bar and tossed Cassie both Raul's wallet and keys, which he had put on the bar to keep them from the mess.

"Go to Brooklyn. The address is on his ID, and in his bedroom is an area rug, under it is a safe, bring the contents here and put them on the fifth floor. Get the cleaner team here to sanitize this mess and tell them to make sure it's a few days before Raul Corstra is found, if he ever is. Trust me, no one will be looking too hard for that swindler. Now get me someone to watch Arthur Ducaine, and between both their companies, we can easily develop this technology and get it to market way ahead of anyone else. The worth of this little venture, Cassie, will more than make up for the measly five million we lost to that deceiving man," Elijah said, pointing to the headless bloody corpse on the floor still gushing blood.

Cassie nodded to him, and Elijah headed for the door of the club; he had to get home. Sunrise was only a half an hour away, and it looked like the best he was going to get for the day was his condo over in Greenwich Village. He just hoped, with the white decor, that he didn't have any blood on him to stain the place; that would upset him more than Raul Corstra's death.

Thank you for reading, and don't miss the next installment of the *Love and Sin Saga*!

ABOUT THE AUTHOR

B.R. Greenley, or Byron Richard Greenley, has been intrigued by both the paranormal and supernatural in both fictional and conventional ways since he was a child. A longtime storyteller who centers on the dark and spiritual side, he brings his debut novel after years of research that seemed to never end.

For a long time, he felt that the world of the demonic and dark sprits seemed to revolve constantly in his life. After three incidents of near-death experiences, he was inspired to begin the work of the first of many forthcoming novels centered on the dark world he's crafted.

He currently lives in NYC with his wife, a practicing Wiccan, where a lot of experiences with the paranormal and supernatural helped to spark his curiosity that helped to craft the dark stories in his mind. When not being focused upon the ghosts and demons in his world, he likes to spend time outdoors, listening to music, reading both novels and historical accounts, or taking moments to watch both movies and shows with his wife that inspire him to write.

Printed in the USA
CPSIA information can be obtained
at www.ICGtesting.com
LVHW040739131023
760664LV00002B/272